# MURDER SHE WROTE; TRICK OR TREACHERY

# TRICK OR TREACHERY

## A Murder, She Wrote Mystery

A Novel by Jessica Fletcher and Donald Bain

based on the Universal television series
created by Peter S. Fischer,
Richard Levinson & William Link

Chivers Press • G.K. Hall & Co.
Bath, England Waterville, Maine USA

This Large Print edition is published by Chivers Press, England, and by G.K. Hall & Co., USA.

Published in 2001 in the U.K. by arrangement with Universal.

Published in 2001 in the U.S. by arrangement with Chivers Press Limited.

U.K. Hardcover  ISBN  0-7540-4564-1  (Chivers Large Print)
U.K. Softcover  ISBN  0-7540-4565-X  (Camden Large Print)
U.S. Softcover  ISBN  0-7838-9496-1  (Nightingale Series Edition)

The text of this Large Print edition is unabridged.
Other aspects of the book may vary from the original edition.

Set in 16 pt. New Times Roman.

Printed in Great Britain on acid-free paper.

**British Library Cataloguing in Publication Data available**

**Library of Congress Cataloging-in-Publication Data**

Bain, Donald, 1935–
  Trick or treachery : a Murder, she wrote mystery : a novel by Jessica Fletcher and Donald Bain.
    p. cm.
  Based on the Universal television series.
  ISBN 0-7838-9496-1 (lg. print : sc : alk. paper)
  1. Fletcher, Jessica (Fictitious character)—Fiction. 2. Women novelists—Fiction. 3. Large type books. I. Murder, she wrote (Television program) II. Title.
  PS3552.A376 T75 2001
  813'.54—dc21                                    2001024384

For Renée Paley

# PROLOGUE

October 27

Dear Matt:

First, thank you for the kind words about my latest novel. There was a point during early September when I doubted whether I'd meet the deadline. Then things opened up, and the final third of the book seemed to write itself.

As for starting the next one, I think I need a month or two of decompression, a time to do some serious thinking and to plan my research.

In the meantime, I've been enjoying my leisure this fall. I think I've mentioned before how people in Cabot Cove seem to take Halloween more seriously than others I've met. It makes for fun actually, lots of parties and pageants and inventive costumes. Strange, though, how the days leading up to this particular Halloween seem different. There's an aura in the air that's unsettling at times. Sounds silly, of course, to hear me speaking this way. You know that I tend to believe only in what I can touch and see, although I've never been so arrogant as to summarily dismiss any phenomenon beyond my ability to personally interact with it. But this

1

Halloween is . . . I'm sounding silly, and I know it. Ghosts and goblins live only in the wonderful imaginations of children.

Thanks again, Matt, for the words of praise. I'll be in touch.

Fondly,

Jessica

As I dropped the letter to my agent, Matt Miller, in the mail slot, I laughed and shook my head. Imagine me actually admitting there might be something to Halloween's mysterious aspects, the ghosts and goblins, witches and cauldrons, and broomsticks that fly. 'Silly,' I said aloud as I stepped outside and got on with my day.

# CHAPTER ONE

'Her name was Hepzibah Cabot. She was the wife of the founder of our town, Winfred Cabot.'

Tim Purdy, Cabot Cove's historian and president of our historical society, stood over a small, weather-worn gravestone in the town's oldest graveyard. Two dozen people, most of them residents, the others tourists, stood in a semicircle across from him as he concluded his annual Halloween tour of Cabot Cove's more infamous historic sites. Tim showed us where murders had taken place: the scene of a scandalous duel between rival candidates for town mayor, in which one had been killed; our stunning, rugged coastline that was a favorite safe haven for pirates plying their trade; and now the burial spot of Hepzibah Cabot, whose murder of her husband and subsequent suicide had been embellished over the decades to create what had become known as the 'Legend of Cabot Cove.'

'Hepzibah was a proud, staunch woman,' Tim continued. 'Her husband, Winfred, was a sea-going man, as most men from here were in those days. He was away at sea for long stretches of time, although the relationship between them was, according to the town's rumor-mongers, such a volatile one that

3

Hepzibah was never especially unhappy during his absences. She was a big woman, tall and raw-boned, who, it's claimed, could cut wood and lay bricks faster and better than any man in town.'

A few people snickered.

'People didn't divorce in those days, and I suppose they would have lived out their lives together if Winfred hadn't taken up with another woman during one of his trips. I'm not sure how Hepzibah found out about it—some accounts claim he told his wife to make her jealous—but the result was violent and bloody. I usually leave out the graphic aspects if children are on the tour, but since we don't have any little ones with us today, I'll say that Hepzibah took an ax to her husband, severing his head and throwing it into the sea from a large rock along the shore. Then she threw herself into the ocean and drowned.'

'A regular Lizzie Borden,' someone said.

'Except that no one has ever denied the facts in this case,' Tim observed. 'She killed her husband and killed herself.'

A man who'd introduced himself and his wife as being from Burlington, Vermont, asked, 'Why did the murder and suicide turn into a legend? Women have killed philandering husbands and then killed themselves before, and still do.'

'True,' Tim said, 'but in those cases, once the principals were dead, that was the end of

4

them. Not so with Hepzibah Cabot. Even today, people claim to see her in various places, wandering on the beach with seaweed streaming from her hair, or right here in this cemetery, staring down at her husband's grave.' Tim pointed to a far corner. 'Townsfolk buried them on opposite sides of the cemetery because of the bad blood between them.'

A woman let out an anguished rush of breath. 'I hope she doesn't decide to show up here this morning,' she said.

Tim laughed. 'Frankly, I keep hoping she does every time I give this annual Halloween tour. Would sure add some drama.'

I observed the others on the tour, especially a man who stood back from the rest. I didn't recognize him, nor did he look like a typical tourist. I judged him to be in his late thirties, perhaps forty. He wore a blue suit that had the rich look of British tailoring, and a vest and tie. He was clean shaven. If it wasn't for his hair, which was pulled back into a ponytail and secured by a leather strap—perhaps an attempt to make himself appear younger—he would have looked very much at home on Wall Street. As Tim led us from the cemetery, the man left in the opposite direction, meandering through the graveyard and stopping to read inscriptions.

I followed the group back to the town dock, where the tour had started.

'I thank you for your interest and patience,'

5

Tim said. 'And a happy, safe Halloween to all.' Halloween was two days away.

I went directly into Mara's Luncheonette, where my friend of many years, Dr. Seth Hazlitt, waited for me. I'd stayed away from Mara's the past few weeks because I was trying to drop a little weight; her blueberry pancakes have been known to add pounds at a single sitting. But Seth convinced me that with winter not far off I'd better start packing in the calories, like a squirrel storing nuts, in order to get through what is often a severe, although for me always enjoyable winter season in Cabot Cove. Seth is generally unhappy when I'm dieting and declining his invitations to join him at Mara's, where calories are celebrated, not counted. He loves to eat; his waistline is testimony to it.

I joined him in a booth.

'Enjoy the tour?' he asked.

'Yes. I hadn't taken it in a while. Tim is wonderful, really knows how to keep a group's interest. But it started to get cold. Why is it always colder in a cemetery than anywhere else? It isn't, of course. The temperature is the same as a block away. But there's always an extra chill.'

Seth laughed. 'Time 'a year, Jessica. All those ghosts and goblins blowin' cold breath on you. Seen this?'

He slid that day's copy of the *Bangor Times* across the table. The headline on page three immediately caught my eye.

## PARANORMAL INVESTIGATOR TARGETS CABOT COVE

'I hate to read things like that,' I said.

'You haven't read the story yet,' he said, pouring sugar into his coffee. 'Let me see the sports page when you're finished.'

I took a break from my pancakes to read the lead story on ghost hunters, and to look at a photo that accompanied it. 'I just saw him,' I said.

'Just saw who?'

'This man, this so-called paranormal investigator. He was on the tour this morning.'

'That so?'

As I read, I became increasingly dismayed.

'This is so irresponsible,' I said.

Seth chuckled. 'Come on now, Jess, you know the media will do anything for a story. This piece of nonsense probably sold lots of newspapers.'

'But it isn't true.'

'True enough,' he said, sitting back, wiping his mouth with a napkin, then dropping it on the table and folding his hands contentedly over his corpulent stomach. 'Can't argue that we got this nut Tremaine livin' in our midst now. Nobody likes havin' him around, but you can't keep a man from openin' an office. Wouldn't be constitutional.'

7

'Yes, I know,' I said, 'but just because someone is claiming that a ghost called the Legend of Cabot Cove will wreak vengeance on the town unless its unhappy spirit is mollified, that shouldn't be the basis for a story that a newspaper treats as fact.'

'Jess, you've dealt with the media enough to know that all it takes is a kernel of an idea, one rumor, and they're off and running. Did you read in the story how Tremaine claims Cabot Cove is the center of the spirit world in New England?'

'Of course I did,' I said, unable to keep the annoyance from my voice. I slapped the newspaper down on the table and shook my head. 'Seth, Lucas Tremaine is already preying on certain individuals in this town. Oh, he's clever, I'll give him that. I've heard he charges "dues" for his society and then swears its members to secrecy so no one is quite sure what he's getting away with. On top of the dues, members pay extra, a lot extra as I hear it, to make contact with their departed loved ones. The man has no shame. Richard Koser told me Tremaine has at least a dozen followers at that center of his out on the old quarry road.'

'If that's all he's got, he won't be in business very long. If you can call ghost hunting a business.'

'He's bilking these people out of their hard-earned money.'

8

'Can't tell people what to spend their money on, Jess. Chances are, when they find they aren't really talkin' to dead relatives, or come to learn after talkin' to them why they never liked 'em in the first place, they'll desert him and that will put an end to his nonsense. That buildin' he's in was practically condemned ten years ago, and it's been sittin' empty ever since. Drew Muscoot tells me it's rotten through and through. He wanted to tear it down to keep from havin' some kids end up in there someday and havin' the ceiling fall on them, but the town board wouldn't go along with him. You'd think they'd listen to the best highway superintendent we've ever had, but you can't always figure how elected officials will think. Go on, finish your pancakes before they get cold.'

I ate in silence, but my mind was working overtime.

Lucas Tremaine had arrived in Cabot Cove two months before, claiming to be a scientific investigator, although he was never specific about what degree he held or where he had studied. His organization, the Society for Paranormal Investigation, or S.P.I., was housed in a building that had once been a notorious road-house. His 'headquarters,' if that's what you could call it, had been in Cabot Cove's inventory of untaxed property ever since the owner skipped town owing everyone, and our civic leaders were evidently happy to rent it to anyone foolish enough to want it.

Shortly after his arrival, Tremaine took a series of small ads in our local newspaper, inviting people to join his allegedly scientific society. People laughed when they heard that Tremaine actually believed in the Legend of Cabot Cove and wanted to make contact with the spirit world. They thought that no one in town would respond to the ads. But a dozen people did, perhaps looking for something new in their lives, or seeking the companionship of like thinkers, or maybe even believing in ghosts the way Tremaine claimed to. No matter what the reason for reasonable people to respond to what was clearly a scam, Tremaine's presence in Cabot Cove had become unsettling. His hints that people in power might be hiding information had caused a few otherwise rational townspeople to begin questioning whether some of our leading citizens were covering up the existence of spirits in Cabot Cove—spirits which, if not appeased, would take their revenge in fearsome ways. That anyone would put even a modicum of credence in Tremaine's maniacal rantings and ravings boggled my mind.

Mara came to the table, a coffeepot in each hand. 'How's breakfast, folks? More coffee, Seth, Jessica?'

'Excellent as usual,' Seth said, pushing his cup in her direction.

'No more for me, thanks,' I said, taking a

10

deep breath to cool my pique.

Mara leaned over the table and filled Seth's cup halfway with decaf, then switched pots and filled it the rest of the way with regular coffee. She looked down the row of booths along the front window overlooking the harbor, and lowered her voice. 'She's been coming in regular since she moved here,' Mara said, nodding at a table in a far corner where a woman sat alone.

'Who is she?' I asked.

'That woman who rented a cottage on Paul Marshall's estate. She's real strange like. She looks at you with those eyes like she's boring a hole right through you.'

'Where did she move from?' Seth asked.

'Somewhere down south.'

'Down south?' I said. 'Florida? Georgia?'

'Don't know for sure. Massachusetts, I think. Salem, Massachusetts,' Mara said.

I laughed. 'I'd hardly call that "down south."'

'Well, it's south of here,' Mara said, chuckling.

'Ayuh, it certainly is south of here. The whole country almost is south of here,' Seth said.

'You didn't like the pancakes this morning, Jess?' Mara asked, pointing to the few scraps I'd left on my plate.

'They were wonderful, Mara, as always, but I've been on a diet and fill up faster than I used to.'

11

Mollified, she wandered off with her coffeepots and stopped two tables away where Mayor Jim Shevlin and his wife were having breakfast with Joe Turco, a young lawyer. Mara's Luncheonette enjoys the advantage of having the best view in Cabot Cove—it's right on the Town Dock—as well as being the gathering place of choice for our village officials. If you want to know what's happening in Cabot Cove, take your meals at Mara's. The reporters from the local newspaper and radio station do. That's how they get most of their leads on breaking news.

I'm willing to bet the reporter from the Bangor paper stops in at Mara's and hears talk about S.P.I. Or, if not here, he could pick it up, along with a bag of doughnuts, at Sassi's Bakery. In small towns like Cabot Cove, the news gets around the old-fashioned way—by mouth. Of course, there's a lot of salting and flouring that gets done to the news when so many cooks are handling the recipe, and sometimes you have to search out the truth, like plucking a bone from the fish chowder. I thought about Lucas Tremaine. What was the truth behind his move to Cabot Cove?

'Ready, Jess?' Seth took a last sip of coffee.

'Yes, I believe so.'

Seth moved to the cash register at the counter, where two uniformed telephone repairmen, one tall and broad, the other short and wiry, were seated on stools, debating the

12

merits of a new fishing lure. Seth clapped one on the shoulder, interrupting the friendly argument.

'You boys find out yet what's causin' the problems with the phones?' he asked. 'My patients say they're still havin' trouble getting through.'

'Sorry, Doc. There's complaints all over town,' the smaller man said. 'We're working on it. Maybe by tomorrow. How do, Mrs. Fletcher?'

'We'll figure it out eventually. We always do,' his colleague added, nodding at me. 'Say, ma'am, Doc, what do you think of this spinner? It's a beauty, ain't it?' He winked at his friend and held out his palm to show us the red-and-silver striped lure with a wicked-looking hook dangling from its end.

'What I see is another office visit if you're not careful with that hook,' Seth said sternly.

'Aw, Doc, you know me and Pete always take the barbs off, give the fish a fair fight.'

Seth grunted, paid, and we stepped outside. It was a splendid October day. I treasure every month in Cabot Cove. It doesn't matter to me if snow is falling and the temperature is below zero, or if midsummer heat and humidity have set in. But there's no doubt about it, October is my favorite month of the year in the town I love so much. We have spectacular fall foliage. The sun shines brightly, but there's a bracing nip in the air that sends me into a frenzy of activity. If I had my way, October would last for six months.

'All set for Halloween?' I asked Seth as we stood outside and breathed in the pristine Maine air.

'The party, you mean?'

'Yes. Have you decided on a costume?'

'Thought I wouldn't wear one,' Seth said.

'Everyone wears a costume to Paul Marshall's annual party,' I said. 'It's one of the rules. You have to come in costume.'

'Seems like a foolish rule to me.'

'Silly rule or not, you don't want to be a spoilsport. Do you want me to find a costume for you?'

'If I have to wear one, you might as well pick it out for me.'

'I'll be happy to do that.'

'What costume are you wearing, Jess?'

'I'm going as The Legend.'

The sound of the door opening caused us to turn. The woman Mara had pointed out to us had left the restaurant and stood on the dock, staring at us. She wore a black duster that swept the ground; a large black pendant in the shape of a cat's face, with glittering red stones of undetermined type for eyes, hung from a silver chain. Her long, flowing white hair gleamed in the sun, but her face was surprisingly youthful, her eyes a startling, piercing blue. Those eyes—something tickled my memory, but I couldn't figure out why. She turned and walked slowly away.

'I see what Mara meant,' I said. 'She has remarkable eyes, like . . . like laser beams.'

'Didn't seem so unusual to me,' Seth said. 'Come on, I'll drive you home.'

'Thanks, but I think I'll walk off those pancakes.'

'Suit yourself.'

He started to leave, then stopped, turned and said, 'Don't be gettin' me any silly kind 'a costume Jess. Keep it simple. Maybe somethin' in the military vein.'

'Simple, huh? Okay, thanks for the tip. A military man you will be this Halloween.'

'Sure you want to go as The Legend? Lucas Tremaine might decide to hunt you down.'

'I don't think I have to worry about that,' I said, smiling. 'I'll just scare him off.'


# CHAPTER TWO

I went home and resumed tasks I'd started a few days ago, filing, paying bills, checking my e-mail and catching up on correspondence. I'd finished my latest novel in mid-September. Writing always fatigues me; if I'm not drained after four or five hours at my word processor, chances are what I've written won't be up to my standards. But this novel had taken a particularly heavy toll on me, and I was

15

relieved when I finished it and shipped it off to Matt Miller in New York.

Whenever I'm closing in on the end of a novel, I invariably let daily chores slip, and once I've written 'The End' on a manuscript, I tackle those things with energy and even pleasure, enjoying the feeling that my house, and my life, are being put back in order. This time, however, I'd opted to take a couple of weeks off, doing nothing except sleeping, enjoying long walks and spending pleasant social time with friends. But the growing piles of paperwork that needed to find a proper place in my files, and the e-mail messages and letters I was determined to answer, eventually put an end to my days of leisure.

By noon, I'd made a good-sized dent in the mountain of work. Then I remembered I'd taken on the responsibility of finding Seth a costume to wear to the Halloween party at Paul Marshall's mansion. We don't have a costume shop in Cabot Cove, and there wasn't time for me to make the trek to Bangor or some other larger city in search of one.

I called my friend Peter Eder, who'd moved to Cabot Cove a year earlier to become the conductor of our flourishing symphony orchestra. Peter had not only quickly whipped the orchestra into fine shape; he'd become deeply involved with a regional theater that had sprung up in Cabot Cove and started to receive substantial notice and good reviews. I tried him at the theater first, but could barely hear the phone ring through the static on the line. I finally reached him at home.

'Hello, Peter, it's Jessica.'

'Hello to you, Jessica. How are you on this splendid fall day?'

'Couldn't be better, although the phone line to the theater could use some help. I tried you there first.'

'Oh, you're getting all that static, too? I've been calling the phone company for weeks now trying to get it fixed. Sorry you had trouble reaching me.'

'Well, I've got you now. Peter, I wonder if you'd do me a favor.'

'If I can.'

'I promised Seth Hazlitt I'd find a costume for him to wear to Paul Marshall's Halloween party. I thought there might be something in the theater's wardrobe room.'

'There probably is. Marcia Davis has done an incredible job of building up that department. She's a scrounger without peer. What kind of costume were you thinking of?'

'Seth said he wanted something military.'

'Wants to relive his World War Two days?'

'Maybe. At any rate, do you know if the wardrobe department includes military uniforms?'

'Sure it does, but I couldn't tell you which ones. Want me to call Marcia? I spoke with her just a little bit ago. She'll be at the theater all afternoon.'

'Would you? I'd really appreciate it.'

I settled back at my desk and resumed working until the phone rang fifteen minutes later.

'Jessica? Jess? Can you hear me? It's Peter.'

A buzz filled my ear, then faded away.

'That's better. I can hear you now.'

'This is really intolerable. I've been calling the phone company, and they just keep patting me on the head, figuratively, of course, and telling me they haven't found the source of the problem, which is pretty apparent.'

'I'm sure they're working on it as best they can,' I said. 'Until this latest problem, service has always been good. Seth and I saw two repairmen in Mara's this morning.'

'They should be out climbing telephone poles,' Peter said with a huff.

'Everyone has to eat.'

'I know, I know. Please don't pay any attention to my grousing. It's just that this whole phone thing has been frustrating.'

'Yes, I know,' I murmured sympathetically.

'I talked with Marcia,' he said, returning to his usual brisk manner. 'She said they have a pretty good selection of military uniforms, World War One, World War Two, Vietnam, the Civil War, even a couple of replicas of Revolutionary times. What do you think Seth would like?'

'Undoubtedly the Revolutionary War

18

uniform. He's a real buff.'

'Well, fitting Seth's front porch might be a bit of a problem. Why don't you go over to the theater and see what's there? I told Marcia you'd be by.'

'Great idea, Peter. Thanks. Hope I didn't intrude on a busy day.'

'No, just fighting with the telephone company and trying to stay ahead of cataloguing scores, making order out of chaos.'

I smiled. What Peter Eder considered chaos would represent pristine orderliness to most of us. He's the neatest man I've ever known.

Because I don't drive, my instinct was to pick up the phone and call the local cab company, which had been taken over five years ago by a lovely Greek family. They'd bought it from the retiring owner and had built it into quite a business, including stretch limousines for longer trips and a minibus for larger groups. But as the sun streamed through my window and created lovely patterns on my desk, I decided it was too nice a day for a taxi. I went to the garage, pulled out my trusty bicycle, hopped on it and headed for the theater.

Marcia Davis was in the lobby when I arrived. She was hanging posters for the next production. She put down her stapler and took me backstage to the wardrobe rooms, where she'd already pulled out all the military uniforms in the inventory and hung them on a

19

rolling garment rack.

'These are wonderful,' I said, fingering each one.

'We haven't done a play with a military theme in a long time, but I believe in being ready in case we do.'

I took a uniform from the rack. 'Revolutionary War?' I asked.

'Yes.'

'This is the British uniform, right?' I said.

The bright red jacket had two sets of brass buttons down the front and braid along the shoulder. 'It looks like it might fit Seth.'

'It is . . . large.'

'British soldiers in the Revolutionary War must have eaten well.'

'It's just a costume, of course, not the real thing,' Marcia said, pulling a pair of white knee-length pants off a hanger. 'But it's authentic. Do you think Seth has white knee socks to go with these?' She laughed.

'I'm not sure, but I know where to buy them. I wonder how he'll feel being on the losing side.'

Marcia's smile turned to a frown. 'If I had a colonist's uniform, I'd give you that. Come to think of it, did the colonists even have a uniform? I hope Seth won't be upset.'

'I was just kidding,' I said. 'May I take it with me?'

'Of course.' Her smile reappeared. 'I know you'll return it in good shape.'

20

'Thanks, Marcia. You made it all very easy.'

'Oh, wait,' she said. 'He'll need the hat, too.' She rummaged through a large carton of hats wrapped in white tissue paper, and extracted a triangular package, pulling off the paper to reveal an ornate tricorn.

'Here you go.'

'What about shoes?' I asked.

'Can't help there, Jess. He'll have to make do with a pair of ordinary black ones.'

Marcia took the red coat off the hanger and folded it over the pants. She put the hat on top, and tucked the stack in a plastic bag that fit neatly in my bike's rear basket.

I had a choice of two routes home. One would take me through the countryside, the other through town. I chose the latter, planning a stop at Charles Department Store to pick up white knee socks for Seth.

I'd reached the center of Cabot Cove when a disturbance at an intersection caught my eye. Being naturally curious—Seth Hazlitt is often dismayed at my inherent and obsessive curiosity—I pedaled closer to where the disturbance was taking place. Lucas Tremaine stood on a bench, addressing a group of bystanders. Gesticulating passionately, his voice rising and falling in concert with the movement of his arms, he'd attracted a small crowd that stood in rapt attention. He was shouting, his words reaching me clearly although I was fifty feet away.

'There is evil afoot in this community, and those of you who fail to realize it will be doomed to suffer the consequences. Yes, you laugh and scoff at the notion that restless spirits are in your midst, but the truth will out. The Legend of Cabot Cove walks. Many have seen her. At night. On the beach. In the cemetery. Which one of you has seen her, or felt her chilling presence, but were afraid to come forward?'

Tremaine pointed at a man in a brown-and-black checked flannel shirt, Artie Sack, an old-timer whose family had been in Cabot Cove for generations. Artie had a reputation for being 'slow'—learning-impaired, it was said. He'd dropped out of school in the eighth grade and become a gardener for several local residents. If Artie's academic abilities were limited, he made up for it by being a savant when it came to plants, flowers and almost anything else having to do with gardening. He could rattle off the Latin and common names of virtually every type of flowering plant, tell you when they were first introduced, and instruct you on how to plant and care for them. Roses were his specialty; the rose garden he'd created for Paul Marshall beside a cottage on his estate was considered to be one of the finest examples in the state of Maine, and photographs of it had appeared in a national home and garden magazine.

Artie Sack lived on Marshall's property, in a

small apartment above a four-car garage. I knew Artie pretty well. I've never been considered someone with a green thumb, and if the property around my house looked pretty in the spring and summer, it was because Artie showed up once a week to make it so. His widowed sister-in-law, who lived in town, worked as a housekeeper for Paul Marshall.

Tremaine spoke directly to Artie, like a sidewalk pitchman who'd found an easy mark, his voice becoming deeper, more urgent. 'The Legend of Cabot Cove is not alone,' he intoned, shaking a finger at Artie, then raising his arms to the sky. 'She is calling her spirit brothers and sisters to a convocation. Here!' He now pointed at the ground. His eyes were full of fire. 'They will descend upon this village in their hundreds, possibly thousands. Their misery will permeate the atmosphere. They will haunt your homes, infect your workplace, creep into your hideaways, wreaking their vengeance on all the citizens of Cabot Cove. Machines will malfunction, food will spoil, traffic will snarl, animals will howl, crime will run rampant through the streets. And unless you do something, ladies and gentlemen, do something now, there will be hell to pay.'

He was roaring now. 'They're coming. You mark my words. The Legend and her brothers and sisters will be here soon. But it's not too late, not yet. I'm here to help you. Together we will see that they are driven out.'

The sound of a siren drowned out Tremaine's next words as Sheriff Mort Metzger pulled up in his black-and-white squad car. 'All right, folks, let's move along now.' Mort's voice boomed out of his vehicle's loudspeaker. He got out and waved the crowd away. I looked around. In the short time I'd been listening, Tremaine's audience had grown. Merchants stood in their shop doorways, their customers spilling out onto the sidewalk. It looked as if all Cabot Cove had stopped what they'd been doing to listen to this madman.

'Sheriff,' Tremaine yelled from his perch, 'this is a legal gathering. Have you never heard of freedom of speech, freedom of assembly? You're tramping on my rights. I demand to be allowed to communicate with these good people.'

'You can communicate all you want,' Mort shouted back, 'but it's public safety I'm concerned about, and you're blocking traffic, not to mention alarming the citizens with your claptrap.'

Tremaine struck a defiant pose. 'See?' he called to the departing crowd. 'The officials in Cabot Cove are afraid of us. They know I'm telling you the truth, but they're hiding the facts from you. It's a cover-up. Don't let them get away with it. Join me.'

Mort took a step toward the bench. Tremaine glared at him before climbing down

24

and thrusting circulars into outstretched hands as he pushed his way through the few remaining listeners. Some teenagers jeered him, and a woman yelled, 'You're nothing but a nut case.'

Her comment caused Tremaine to stop and turn. I feared he would physically attack her.

Instead, he muttered something I couldn't hear, then stalked away.

The audience slowly dispersed, and Cabot Cove's village center, as we refer to downtown, resumed its usual peaceful mien. I looked for Artie Sack, but he'd disappeared.

When I entered Charles Department Store, it was buzzing with gossip about Tremaine and his predictions of dire happenings. I crossed the creaky wooden floor, skirted the wooden display cabinets, waved to the group gathered at the cashier's desk and found my way to the men's department in the back, where bins of socks were located.

'Exciting afternoon, huh, Jessica?' said David Raneri, one of the store's owners as he came down the aisle with an armload of sweaters.

'I don't know if I'd call it exciting exactly. Disturbing comes closer to mind.'

'You're the writer, so I'll let you pick the words,' he said, grinning.

Richard Koser turned from the counter where he'd been examining a green cardigan and plucked a deep blue one from the pile in

David's arms. Besides being a wonderful commercial photographer—he'd shot most of the photos for my books' dust jackets— Richard was one of Cabot Cove's acknowledged gourmet cooks. 'Thanks, Dave,' Richard said. 'Just the right color.' He held it up to his chest. 'What do you think, Jess?'

'Looks perfect to me,' I said.

'Told you about that maniac, didn't I?' Richard continued. 'He'll probably get a good audience, too. P. T. Barnum was right, about a sucker being born every minute.'

David turned to me. 'Can I help you find something, Jess?'

'I hope so. I need a pair of long white socks.'

'For you?'

'Actually, no. They're for Seth Hazlitt.'

Richard and David exchanged amused glances.

'Not for his everyday use,' I quickly added. 'It's for his Halloween costume. Paul Marshall's annual party.'

'What's Doc going as,' Koser asked, 'the lead dancer from *The Nutcracker*?' Richard could be as acerbic as he was talented with a camera.

'No,' I said, 'he's going as a Revolutionary War soldier.'

'An officer, I assume,' said Koser. 'Doc Hazlitt would never be content as an enlisted man.'

'I think it's an officer's uniform,' I said. 'I

26

got his costume from Marcia Davis at the theater. I need the long white socks to finish it off.'

'Come with me,' David said, setting down the sweaters on a table. 'Women's section.'

In all my travels I have never encountered a store quite like Charles's. It seems there is nothing they don't have on hand—nothing. That David immediately handed me a pair of long white socks wasn't at all surprising.

'Think they'll fit Seth?' I asked.

'It's the biggest pair we have,' David said. 'Lots of elastic. They'll expand to fit almost everyone. I think he'll manage to get into them.'

I followed David to the checkout counter and stood in line behind the woman Mara had pointed out at breakfast that morning. She was in the process of paying for her purchases—a pointed shovel with a long handle, a sturdy rake and gardening gloves.

'Need help out to the car with those, Ms. Swift?' David asked her.

'No, thank you,' she said flatly. 'I can manage just fine.'

The woman—I now knew her last name—gathered the garden tools to her chest and walked to the front door.

'She's new in town, isn't she?' I asked.

'Yes,' David said. 'Matilda Swift. She's renting one of the cottages on Paul Marshall's estate.'

'So I've heard.'

I turned from him and looked about the store.

'Something wrong?' David's brother, Jim, asked from behind the counter.

'No, I . . . I thought someone might have opened a window. I suddenly feel cold.'

'We've been complaining all day it's too hot,' Jim Raneri said, laughing.

'The Rose Cottage,' David said as he placed the white socks in a bag. 'She's renting the Rose Cottage on Marshall's estate.

'She's lucky,' I said. 'That garden is spectacular.'

'I know. Well, Jess, there you are. Doc Hazlitt's all set for the party. Still cold?'

'No. It came as fast as it went. Thanks, fellas. You always come through with what I need.'

*     *     *

The vision of Lucas Tremaine preaching on that corner stayed with me through the rest of the day and into the evening. There's always something disquieting about someone who espouses destructive thoughts because even though most folks might view such people for what they are, unbalanced zealots, they will always find some following. My hope was that Mr. Tremaine would fail in his enterprise and simply go away—not a particularly generous thought, but one that accurately reflected my feelings.

I also reflected on the sudden chill I'd experienced in the department store. If I didn't know better, the rush of cold air that seemed to have engulfed me had come from Ms. Swift, as though she was a refrigerator whose door had been opened. Warmth returned the minute she left the store.

I had a quiet dinner alone at home—clam chowder, crusty French bread and a salad topped with shavings of Parmesan cheese—and went to bed early. The problem was that someone else hadn't gone to bed quite as early. The phone rang. I sleepily picked up the receiver. The line was clear.

'Hello?'

'Hi there, Mrs. F. Did I wake you?'

'As a matter of fact, Mort, you did, but that's all right,' I said, throwing off the covers, sitting up and wriggling back to rest against the headboard.

'Just wanted to see if you had any idea what costume I might wear to Paul Marshall's Halloween party.'

'You, too?'

'What do you mean by that?'

'I picked up a costume for Seth today.'

'What did you get him?'

'He's going to be a British soldier from the Revolutionary War.'

Mort chuckled. 'He wouldn't know one end

29

of a musket from the other.'

'Be that as it may, he's going as a "lobsterback." I got the costume at the theater. You still haven't decided what to wear?'

'Nope. Maureen's going as that singer, Cher. Got herself a whole outfit complete with a long black wig from a mail order costume place down in New York.'

'Good for her. At least she was thinking ahead.' The sound of static began to crackle softly under our conversation.

'I thought I'd just come in my sheriff's uniform,' Mort said, raising his voice. 'But Maureen says that's not a costume.'

'It would be on someone who isn't a sheriff,' I said, matching his volume, 'but it isn't for you. Why don't you go as a soldier, too? Marcia Davis has a wonderful selection of uniforms at the theater. You could go as a World War Two doughboy, or someone from the Civil War.'

'That's a good idea. Of course, I wouldn't want to step on Seth's toes.'

'I'm sure you wouldn't unless you wore a red jacket and white knee pants.' The static was louder now.

'Haven't worn knee pants since I was five,' Mort shouted into the phone. 'Well, sorry to have woken you, Mrs. F. I'll check in with Marcia tomorrow morning.'

'You do that, Mort,' I called out. 'Say hello to Maureen for me. Good night.'

I smiled as I sank down and drew up the covers. Cabot Cove was such a wonderful place to live, and I had such dear friends. But my final thought was of Lucas Tremaine and his speech downtown that afternoon, and of the strange lady, Ms. Swift, who was now a member of our community. My dreams reflected it—they were not pleasant dreams. I woke early in the morning groggy and out of sorts.

## CHAPTER THREE

'Jess, it's Matt.'

'Hello, Matt. Getting a call from you is always a nice way to start the day.'

'Wish all my clients felt that way. Jess, what's this I hear about a Cabot Cove legend?'

'Legend? Oh, you mean *that* legend.' I laughed. 'How did you hear about it?'

'It's in this morning's paper, something about a guy named Tremaine coming to Cabot Cove to drive this legend away.'

'What paper?'

'The *New York Daily News.*'

'Oh, my. I didn't think the story would interest anyone outside of Maine. It's all silliness, Matt. The legend goes back two hundred years. Hepzibah Cabot was the wife of the founder of Cabot Cove. She killed her husband when she discovered he'd been unfaithful to her, and then threw herself off a cliff into the sea. Even today people claim to see her in various places, wandering on the beach with seaweed streaming from her hair, or in the cemetery near her husband's grave. Cabot House, her home, is now the headquarters of our historical society. Although The Legend has never been seen there, local history buffs love to retell the story every year, especially to the children who visit Cabot House. Of course they skip the reason she killed her husband.'

'Raises a lot of goose bumps with the little ones, I bet,' Matt said.

'Yes, it does. Children so enjoy ghost stories, and it seems to help interest them in history.'

'Well, Jess, The Legend is an amusing tale, but it doesn't seem to be especially newsworthy.'

'It wasn't until recently. About two months ago, a man named Lucas Tremaine arrived and claimed to have made contact with The Legend. He's preaching—yes, that's what I'd call it, preaching—that The Legend is about to raise her pretty head and wreak havoc on us, and that only he can stave it off.'

'Can he?'

'Can he? Matt! There is no Legend, and Mr. Tremaine is a con man. Besides claiming he's our savior, he's established quite a little cult for himself, putting the gullible in touch with deceased loved ones in the spirit world—for sizable fees, I might add.'

'Could be a book in it.'

'Maybe, but not from this writer.'

'Just thinking out loud. Any plans to head down to New York this fall?'

'None at the moment, but I'd like to,' I said, glancing at my watch. 'Have to run, Matt. I'm due at a meeting and rehearsal in a half hour.'

'Meeting? Rehearsal? About what?'

'Our annual children's Halloween pageant.'

'That's right. Halloween is just a few days away. Perfect time for spirits to come out of the woodwork and—Jess? Can you hear me?'

'There goes the phone again. We've been having nothing but trouble with the lines all over town.'

'I can barely hear you.'

'Good-bye, Matt. We'll talk when they fix things.'

I hung up and considered placing a call to the phone company, but realized it wouldn't accomplish anything. I'd already called a half-dozen times since the trouble began. Nothing to be gained by telling the company what it already knew.

The meeting about the pageant was scheduled to begin at ten at the elementary school. I had plenty of time and decided to walk. It was a typical fall day, the sky cobalt blue and without a cloud, a bright sun hurling shafts of light through the brilliant yellows of the sugar maples. It was truly a day to buoy my spirits, as though they needed uplifting. It was, as Seth Hazlitt would describe it, a 'fat day.'

I took the shore route, stopping occasionally to take a deep breath of the bracing salt air and to admire the millions of dancing ripples on the ocean's surface created by a stiff onshore breeze. I closed my eyes and allowed the sun to play over my face. When I opened them, I realized I was no longer alone. Standing there was Erica Marshall, daughter of Paul Marshall, at whose lavish home we would gather for our annual grown-up Halloween party.

'Hello there, Erica. Fabulous day, isn't it,' I called out as I strode toward her.

She'd been looking down, examining the sand at the margin as the foam edged close to her shoe, her arms tightly crossed. Every time I see Erica Marshall, the term 'delicate' comes to mind. She is doll-like, extremely slender and finely etched, her facial features like a perfectly carved cameo, hands and feet appropriately tiny. She couldn't be taller than five feet, perhaps even an inch shy of that. Silky brown hair that curves under at her jaw adds to the overall impression of beauty in miniature.

She glanced up at the sound of my voice, a startled look on her young face.

'Sorry,' I said, stopping a few feet away. 'Didn't mean to disturb your thoughts.'

'Oh, that's all right, Mrs. Fletcher.' Judging from her frown, her thoughts might not have been pleasant.

'Taking some time off to appreciate this beautiful day?' I inquired. I knew Erica worked for her father in some capacity at his factory.

'It is beautiful, isn't it,' she said sadly, looking out to sea. 'No, I just took a little detour on my way to the office.'

'How's your dad? Getting ready for the party?'

She looked as though she might break into tears. I wondered if the annual party at Paul Marshall's estate, the first social gathering there since the tragic fire that took the life of her father's partner, Anthony Scott, was distressing her. Perhaps the upcoming year anniversary of that melancholy event was in her thoughts. I was also aware through the town's efficient grapevine that father and daughter had been estranged at times, although the reasons why seemed to evade those in the know.

She started to stammer. 'Oh . . . oh, everyone's fine, thanks. Yes . . . yes, getting ready for the party.'

'Well,' I said, annoyed I hadn't been sensitive enough to couch my cheery greeting. 'I'd better be going. I'll see you there, dear.'

'Bye, Mrs. Fletcher.'

I spent the rest of my walk to the

elementary school reflecting on that terrible accident a year ago.

Anthony Scott had been Paul Marshall's partner in a manufacturing and mail order business featuring a line of rugged outerwear that was popular with sportsmen. The business had been profitable for years . . . until competitors stepped up their sales efforts and chipped away at Marshall-Scott Clothing's share of the market. That's when Tony Scott's scientific mind went to work. He was the technical genius of the partnership, Paul Marshall the marketing and sales expert.

Scott had been working on a new insulating material to line their clothing that he claimed was far superior to Thinsulate and other materials used by the competition. Their work had even been written about in the business press. The problem, again according to scuttlebutt around town, was that Scott's invention, known as 'BarrierCloth,' was too flammable to meet federal safety standards. Scott had been working day and night in a small laboratory at one end of the main manufacturing building to correct the problem in time to introduce the new line the following spring. But on Halloween night one year ago, while the party was in full swing at Marshall's house, and while Scott worked into the night, a terrible fire destroyed the lab. Scott was burned beyond recognition.

What stuck in my mind as I turned the

corner and headed for the school was the funeral that was held for him . . .

*     *     *

It was a rainy day last year when the body of Anthony Scott was put to rest in the small cemetery adjacent to Paul Marshall's property, Cabot Cove's oldest final resting place of Hepzibah and Winfred Cabot and others who'd lived during the town's formative stages. Because it is so small and crowded, larger cemeteries in other areas of the county are now utilized.

It could be said that Anthony Scott was a stereotypical scientist, introverted and absorbed in whatever he was working on at the moment, although he and his partner had been generous supporters of Cabot Cove's civic activities. Scott's nonworldly approach to life was the subject of good-natured humor. Holding a conversation with him was often difficult because his thoughts seemed always to be elsewhere. And he was accident prone, not surprising for someone who seemed incapable of focusing on where he was, or where he was going.

I remember one incident when Tony was almost run over in the center of town. The light had turned green for cars, and this particular driver, one of our librarians, proceeded through the intersection. Tony

Scott, his mind elsewhere, casually stepped into the intersection and came within an inch of being struck by her car. To the driver's surprise, Tony claimed she'd deliberately tried to hit him. He even went so far as to tell the officer who came to the scene that it wasn't the first time his enemies had attempted to run him over. His claim was dismissed by the amused officer, who knew of Tony's reputation as an eccentric. The incident was forgotten.

Another time, while Tony was walking through the woods during a rainy windstorm, a large branch broke away, landed on his shoulder and broke it. He told the nurses and doctor in the emergency room that someone had obviously sawed through the limb just enough for it to fall and hit him. 'He's so paranoid,' one of the E.R. nurses commented over coffee at Mara's the next morning, laughing.

'He's just an absentminded inventor,' her tablemate said. 'Like Einstein. They're all that way.'

Tony Scott was a dark-haired man, small in both height and build, and wore thick glasses over large blue eyes. His clothes served almost as a uniform: wrinkled chino pants, sweaters with holes in the elbows and tan work boots with thick soles. I didn't know him well; I don't think many people did. He was a widower and lived alone in one of the cottages owned by his partner—a simple lifestyle that seemed perfectly suited to him.

I did know that Scott had a son, Jeremy, who'd gone to live with his mother after she and Tony had separated—it was my understanding they'd never divorced. Mrs. Scott had died when Jeremy was in college, and he'd elected to stay where they were living, somewhere in California, and hadn't returned to Cabot Cove until his father's funeral. He was thirty at the time.

'I'm so sorry about your father, Jeremy. He was a fine man, and I understand, quite an inventor,' I said as we stood in Paul Marshall's baronial living room after returning from the cemetery.

'He certainly was,' Jeremy replied. 'He had an incredible mind for technical things.'

Jeremy Scott was a handsome young man, considerably taller than his father, and dressed in a conservative suit and tie appropriate to any corporate boardroom. He had inherited his father's blue eyes, but his hair, worn short, was the color of beach sand. He had a pleasant smile that put you immediately at ease. Like many young executives of his generation, he'd taken to smoking cigars. This day he held an unlighted one between his fingers. I noticed it had a distinctive wrapper.

'That's a Cuban cigar, isn't it?' I commented. 'Aren't they illegal in this country?'

He laughed. 'My only vice, I'm afraid,' he said, 'and yes, illegal. Friends of mine get them through a source in Prague. No harm done. We should have normal relations with Cuba anyway. Mind if I light up?'

'Not as long as anyone else doesn't.'

I watched him carefully snip off the end of the long brown cigar and light it with a cigarette lighter, careful to keep the flame from actually touching it. He took a satisfied drag and smiled.

'What have you been doing with yourself?' I asked, happy the smoke drifted away from me.

'Working in advertising,' he said, sipping a soft drink.

'Oh? An agency?'

'No, in-house for a large computer firm. I'm leaving there.'

'A better offer?'

'You might say that. I'm coming back to Cabot Cove to work for Dad's company.'

'Marshall-Scott Clothing? That's wonderful.'

'My dad would think so. He always wanted me to join the firm. Mr. Marshall wanted that, too, but I was stubborn—wanted to be on my own, not follow in Dad's footsteps. Now, I think I owe it to him to help make his invention, BarrierCloth, successful.'

'Well, Jeremy, I think that's wonderful news. Welcome back. I know your father would be very proud of you. Where will you be living?'

'Here in Paul's house until I find something

else. He's been very generous with me in many ways, Mrs. Fletcher, including giving me the master guest suite on the top floor.'

'Not one of the cottages?' I asked, thinking that the Rose Cottage in which his father had lived was probably available.

'No. Paul decided to completely renovate Dad's place. He's in the process of gutting it. Besides, I sort of like living here in the main house. It's so big I never see Paul, or anyone else for that matter. I feel like lord of the manor.'

I laughed. 'I understand what you mean,' I said. 'It certainly is an impressive house. Mansion would be more apt, I suppose. He moves fast, doesn't he, your new boss?'

'How so?'

'The Rose Cottage. Tearing it apart so quickly. It was so beautiful the way it was.'

'He's decisive, that's for sure. The outside, with all the roses, is great, but Paul says the inside became pretty shabby. Anyway, if I do decide to move out of this house, there might be another cottage coming up for rent on the property in a few months. The family in it is talking about leaving. In the meantime—'

'In the meantime you'll enjoy your host's hospitality.'

'My boss's hospitality.'

Our conversation ended when Paul Marshall's daughter, Erica, joined us.

'Hi,' Jeremy said. 'I was just telling Mrs.

Fletcher that I'll be staying in Cabot Cove and working for your father. I really appreciate his taking me into the business.'

'Oh, yes, my generous, compassionate father,' Erica said. Her words were kind, her tone not quite so benevolent.

Jeremy picked up on it. 'Now, now, Little Ricky,' he said, smiling. 'Still jealous of me?'

Erica blushed. 'Please don't call me that. I'm not a kid anymore.'

'Last time I saw you, you were. "My how you've grown." Isn't that the usual line?'

'Do you have to smoke that vile cigar?' she said.

'Have one with me,' he said, laughing. 'Cigar smoking is all the rage with young women these days.'

They excused themselves and walked away, and I couldn't help but think they made an attractive couple. Erica was just a child when Jeremy went to live with his mother in California, but here she was all grown-up and beautiful. I doubted Jeremy still saw her as a kid sister.

\*     \*     \*


And here it was a year later. Another Halloween to tickle the fancy of Cabot Cove's children, and its adults, too, Tony Scott's death now an unfortunate memory.

I entered the school and went to the

42

auditorium, where the meeting and rehearsal were being held. Our mayor, Jim Shevlin, was there along with a dozen other government, civic and business leaders. Among many reasons I love Cabot Cove, the enthusiastic involvement of its citizens ranks high on my list. Beth Mullin, who with her husband, Peter, owned the Olde Tyme Floral Shop, gave a report on ticket sales for that evening's pageant. 'Almost sold out,' she said happily, 'just a handful of tickets left.'

'That's great,' Warren Wilson said. 'We'll buy up any unsold tickets.'

'That's not necessary,' answered town attorney Ralph Mackin. 'Marshall-Scott Clothing has been more than generous already.'

Wilson had moved from Vermont to Cabot Cove two years ago to become vice president of Marshall-Scott Clothing, responsible for the company's manufacturing and administrative operations. Paul Marshall, whose generosity was well known to everyone in town, had added to Wilson's duties the role of community relations director. In that capacity, he'd become a highly visible presence in town, showing up at virtually every meeting, particularly when charitable events were involved.

Wilson, a beefy, muscular man whose hair was prematurely abandoning him, waved his hand and laughed. 'You know our company's motto, Ralph. "An involved company is a good

43

company." Paul Marshall feels, and I certainly agree, that supporting our kids is one of the most important things we can do for Cabot Cove.'

'And it's deeply appreciated, as always,' Mayor Shevlin said.

As the discussion at the rear of the auditorium drifted on to other matters, I wandered down to the front, where the high school's drama teacher was putting finishing touches on a scene from the pageant. The children, dressed in a variety of Halloween related costumes, were adorable as they played the roles of witches. A large black pot containing dry ice sent what looked like steam into the air as two little girls, wearing large black hats that kept slipping off their small heads, pretended to stir the witches' brew. The teacher, Pat Hitchcock, noticed me.

'Hi, Jessica,' she said.

'Hi, Pat. Everything shaping up for tonight?'

'I think so,' she said, directing a stream of air at an errant wisp of hair. 'It always seems to come together at the last minute.'

'No small thanks to you,' I said.

A little boy in an orange goblin costume interrupted from the stage. 'I have to go to the bathroom, Mrs. Hitchcock.'

Pat smiled. 'Nature calls even for goblins, Jessica. Excuse me.'

I took a seat near the stage and turned to see the others who were still meeting at the back. Warren Wilson was an interesting man, I thought. He was a bachelor, which made him fair game for rumors about his romantic involvements. Not a few single women had designs on Warren, dropping off casseroles or cakes with his landlady in hopes of impressing him with their culinary skills. But for more than a year the woman most frequently linked to Warren had been Erica Marshall, the proverbial boss's daughter. They'd been seen together socially on a number of occasions, although some claimed that all was not well between them. But that could simply have been the sour reflections of a lady whose efforts were going unrewarded.

My reverie was interrupted when two women took seats in the row behind me and began an animated conversation. At first, I was irritated by their rudeness, talking while the rehearsal was still going on, but then I heard a name that grabbed my attention, and I tuned in to what they were saying.

'Did you hear those dogs last night? Gave me the willies.'

'I know, I know. Our Buster certainly heard 'em. He started howling to wake the dead.'

'That's what Tremaine said was comin', you know—dogs running wild, machines not working right and rampant crime.'

'It's already here. Peggy Johnson told me someone stole John's flannel shirt right off her clothesline last week. And Hap Gormley's car wouldn't start after the concert, and it had been working just fine till then.'

'It must be because of her. All kinds of odd things have been happenin' since that strange lady—Matilda Swift, is it?—moved here.'

I rejoined my friends at the rear of the theater.

'Well, that about covers everything,' Mayor Shevlin said. 'Unless anyone has something else to add.'

'Nothing from me,' Wilson said. 'Have to get back to the office.'

'Once again, Warren, we owe you and the company a debt of gratitude for your generous support of the pageant,' Shevlin said. 'Please extend our thanks to Mr. Marshall.'

I left the school with Wilson.

'See you at the party?' he asked as he unlocked the door of his car, parked directly in front of the school.

'Wouldn't miss it,' I said.

'Good. Paul is pulling out all the stops. The company people will all be wearing the same costume.'

'That's a new approach. What will you be coming as?'

'We're all coming as moose. Mooses? Meese? This is Maine, after all.' He laughed. 'Paul had the costumes specially made in Boston.'

'You were right the first time, Warren. The plural of moose is moose. I look forward to

46

seeing them.'

As he extended his hand, I noticed the back of his right one had been scratched. 'Those are nasty scratches,' I said.

'Damn cat,' he said, looking at his hand. 'We've had a woman move into one of the cottages on Paul Marshall's estate, the Rose Cottage.'

'So I've heard,' I said.

'She's got a black cat with a mean disposition. If I'd known what a nasty critter he is, I wouldn't have tried to pick him up when I was down at the cottage the other day. They say animals take on the personality of their owners, Mrs. Fletcher. It's true in this case. The cat and its owner are both nasty creatures.'

'Well, I wouldn't know about that,' I said. 'Take care, Warren.'

'You, too, Mrs. Fletcher.'

I decided to stop by Mara's Luncheonette for coffee and to see what other news was making the rounds. I'd reached the parking lot and was heading for the door when the loud sound of a revving engine caused me to turn. Matilda Swift backed her automobile from its spot. It was a long black car shined to a mirror gloss. As it moved away, I saw for the first time another occupant, a big black cat with a piercing gaze, sitting on the rear shelf, glaring at me. Although it wasn't a particularly cool day, and I was dressed warmly, a sudden chill went through me.

'Coffee, Jess?' Mara asked after I'd taken a booth.

'What?'

'Coffee? You okay?'

'Okay? Oh, sure. I'm fine. Just chilled, that's all. Winter's in the air. Clam chowder, please, and make it hot. Very hot.'

# CHAPTER FOUR

The chill I woke up to the next morning had nothing to do with large black cats with piercing eyes, or a lady named Matilda Swift. It had to do with a cold front that had barreled through Cabot Cove during the night, dropping the temperature close to freezing.

After showering, dressing in layers and bringing my plants in from the patio in the event we got down to the frost level, I spent the morning finishing up my leftover paperwork. After a late lunch, I headed off for town, not with any specific destination in mind, but more to get the blood flowing. As often happens, I ended up wandering into police headquarters, where I knew Mort Metzger, our sheriff, usually had a pot of relatively decent coffee brewing. As an admitted 'coffee snob,' I choose where to have my coffee with care. A year ago, I wouldn't have gone near Mort's station house brew. But after I complained enough, he allowed me to give him a lesson in coffee making, and let me choose which blends to use. As a result, the quality had improved considerably, enough to satisfy my finicky palate.

I paused outside his office when I saw he wasn't alone, but he waved me in. Seated across the desk from him were Ed and Joan Lerner, relative newcomers to Cabot Cove who'd retired here after completing distinguished careers in education. I'd attended a welcoming party for them at the Unitarian-Universalist church, where I learned that one of their daughters, Liz, was a minister in Maryland; a second daughter, Jenny, a social psychologist, lived in Pittsburgh.

The Lerners had immediately become an integral part of the town's social and civic life, throwing a Bastille Day party at their home not long after moving in, and establishing a play-reading group that quickly became popular.

'Don't want to interrupt anything,' I said.

'We were just about to leave,' Joan said.

'The Lerners were saying how flattered they were to be invited to Paul Marshall's Halloween party,' Mort said, 'being new to town and all.'

'We used to throw our own Halloween party each year,' Ed said, 'but I understand Mr. Marshall's puts most gatherings to shame. We wouldn't want to compete with that.'

'It is lavish,' I said.

Joan laughed. 'If we don't have a Halloween party, we'll just have to find another excuse for a bash. Canadian Bank Day. Boxing Day. Bring Your Daughter to Work Day.'

They stood to leave.

'Now, don't you be concerned, folks,' Mort said, ushering them out. 'I'll look into it.'

'See you at the pageant tonight?' I asked.

'Wouldn't miss it,' said Joan. 'Or the party.'

'Judging from them,' I said to Mort when they were gone, 'retirement doesn't necessarily mean slowing down.'

'That's the way it ought to be.' He sat down behind his desk again and picked up his pen. 'They're good people, Mrs. F.,' he said, jotting a note on his pad and putting the report aside. 'They were at a function down at the Unitarian Fellowship last night and overheard some grumblings concerning Tremaine and his activities. He's made a lot of enemies, that one. There's some who're threatening to take matters into their own hands. The Lerners don't like the man, but they don't want to see his civil rights trampled on either.'

'I know,' I said. 'It's easy to support freedom of speech when you agree with the speaker—much harder when you don't.'

'As long as Tremaine doesn't break any laws, there's not anything I can do about him. I'm not real worried about the threats.

Probably just some hotheads shooting their mouths off. But I'll nose around town later. Appreciate it if you'd keep an ear out, too. Coffee, Mrs. F? I just made a fresh pot.'

'Love a cup.'

With two steaming mugs in front of us, I asked whether things were quiet on the crime front.

'Ayuh,' he said, Maine-speak for yes. 'Pretty much so. Got one drunk back in a cell still sleepin' it off and looks like we might have a laundry bandit on the loose. Mrs. Johnson reported a missin' shirt, and Aggie Taylor complained someone walked off with a pair of skivvies she left dryin' on the porch. Other than that, and the Lerners' concerns, everything's pretty quiet.'

'I'll drink to that,' I said, raising my mug.

Our moment of celebratory reverie was shattered when one of Mort's deputies, Wendell Watson, barged through the door. 'Got a nine-one-one, Sheriff,' he said.

'What's up?'

'Out to Paul Marshall's place. Kid missing from one of the cottages.'

'Missing kid? What kid?'

'Don't know. Marie says the woman's hysterical. Name's Wandowski.'

'Robert and Lauren Wandowski rent one of Paul's cottages,' I said. 'They have a little girl.'

Mort jumped up and grabbed his tan Stetson from where it hung from a set of

51

moose antlers, then headed for the door.

'Mind if I tag along?' I asked.

'Wouldn't matter if I did. Come on.'

*      *      *

When we pulled up in front of the Wandowski cottage, the parents of the child were waiting in front of a compact car, the motor running. Mort and Wendell got out and approached them. I remained in the squad car with the window down.

'Afternoon,' Mort said. 'What's goin' on, folks? Got a report says your youngster is missin'. Fill me in.'

Bob and Lauren started talking at once.

Mort held up his hand. 'Easy, now,' he said. 'One at a time.'

The father spoke. 'Julie is gone. That's our daughter, she's eight. My wife called me at work. I just got here. School let out early today. Kids had just a couple a' hours this morning.'

'A teacher conference,' Lauren said.

'Julie never made it home,' Bob said. 'She's disappeared. She's been kidnapped.'

'Let's not jump to conclusions,' Mort said, reaching in the window and turning off the engine of the compact. 'Might be she decided to stop off someplace, see a friend.' He handed the keys to the father.

'Julie wouldn't do that without telling me,'

Lauren said, glancing at her husband.

'She knows better,' Bob Wandowski added sternly.

'Well, then,' Mort said, 'let's take a walk, backtrack along the route your daughter always takes to school, and see if we can learn anything. One of you stay here in case she comes back or calls.'

A teary Lauren Wandowski agreed to remain behind as Mort, Wendell and Bob set off on foot. I got out of the car and joined them. The trail we took passed through a small spruce grove. When we emerged into a clearing, the Rose Cottage came into view, a hundred yards ahead. A black car was parked alongside it. A five-foot-high wall curved toward the cottage, the remnants of summer roses clinging to its red-brick façade. Artie Sack, the gardener, was spreading mulch at the base of the rose bushes in preparation for a cold winter. I waved, and he waved back. A black cat—probably the same scary animal I'd seen in the back of Matilda Swift's car—was curled up atop the brick wall, its yellow eyes following Artie's labors.

'How are you, Artie?' I called.

'Doin' good, doin' good,' he replied. The cat jumped onto his shoulders as I approached.

'Ooh! Doesn't that hurt?' I asked, watching the cat dig its paws into him.

'This little guy? This little guy?' Artie Sack had a habit of saying things twice. He pulled the cat into his arms and stroked the black head, scratching behind the cat's ears, eliciting a loud purr. 'He couldn't hurt anyone, even if he wanted to. This is a nice cat, nice cat, not like them barn cats.'

'What are we doing here?' Bob growled, drawing my attention away from Artie.

'That's Ms. Swift's home,' I said, pointing to the Rose Cottage and moving back to our little group. 'Maybe she's seen your daughter.'

'That witch!' Bob muttered.

'Witch?' I said.

'Just ask around. Nothing but trouble in town since she came,' he spat. 'We've been thinking of leaving for some time now. Cabot Cove isn't what it used to be. Too many upstarts and weirdos moving in—like her.'

The venom in his voice took me aback. I was about to ask whether he had a reason for his obvious hatred of Matilda Swift, a tangible problem to cause him to speak so ill of her, when the door to the cottage opened. The woman in question stepped outside, followed by a little girl eating a large cookie.

'Julie!' her father shouted, breaking into a run toward them. The girl came around from behind Matilda and waved. 'Hi, Daddy,' she chirped, running to him. He scooped her up in his arms, grabbing the cookie and flinging it to the ground.

' 'Morning, Ms. Swift,' Mort said, tipping his hat.

54

Wandowski lowered his daughter, keeping a hand on her shoulder, and glared at Matilda.

The woman wore an ankle-length white gauze dress and a large pendant with a bronze cat's face against a circular black background. Her expression was quizzical.

'What the hell are you doing with my daughter?' Wandowski snarled.

'Why, we were baking cookies,' Matilda said, frowning in response to his angry tone.

'Are you all right?' Wandowski leaned down to his daughter.

'I'm fine, Daddy. Mrs. Swift asked if I wanted to help them and I—'

'Go home,' her father roared. 'Now!'

The child looked as though she might cry, but managed to hold back the tears as she ran away from us in the direction of the spruce grove.

Wandowski turned on Matilda. 'How dare you kidnap my daughter!'

'I didn't kidnap her,' Matilda said quietly. 'She's such a nice little girl and I was baking cookies and thought—'

'I want her arrested for kidnapping and child endangerment,' Wandowski shouted at Mort.

'Well, now, Mr. Wandowski, I don't think that's warranted. Looks like no harm was done here.'

'You refuse to arrest her?' Wandowski was growing red in the face.

'I suppose you could say that. Now calm down. Your daughter looked happy and healthy enough. Didn't appear she was bein' held against her will. Don't blame you for bein' upset with her for not goin' straight home from school, but that's about the only thing here I can see needs addressing.'

Wandowski turned again to Matilda. 'You come near my daughter again—you come within a hundred yards of her—and I'll take care of you myself.'

'Careful with that sort a' threat, Mr. Wandowski,' Mort said. 'I don't like that brand of talk.'

Wandowski's nostrils flared, and he seemed poised to say something else. Instead, he stalked away, mumbling under his breath.

When he was gone, Mort said to Matilda, 'I'm sure you didn't mean nothin' wrong havin' the girl come in to bake cookies, Ms. Swift, but it might be a good idea to give that whole family a wide berth for a while.'

'Thank you for your advice,' she replied coolly. 'If you don't mind, I'll get back to my baking now. Can't believe such a ruckus over baking cookies. There's something wrong with that man, you know.' The intensity in her icy blue eyes conflicted with what I considered false sweetness in her voice.

'I'm sure he was just upset and worried about his child. He'll probably be embarrassed about this scene by tomorrow,' I said, not entirely sure that would be the case.

Matilda stared at me; I felt as though she'd physically penetrated my body. 'Not that one,' she said, the sweetness of tone now gone. She stepped back inside the cottage.

Mort, Wendell and I returned to where Mort's official car was parked. Robert Wandowski's car was gone.

'You get the feelin', Mrs. F, that this won't be the last trouble we see with Ms. Swift?'

'I don't know about that, Mort, but I do wonder what the girl meant when she said that Mrs. Swift asked if she wanted to help *them*.'

'She said that?'

'Yes.'

'I didn't pick up on that. Good thing Julie's father didn't know there was someone else in the cottage,' Mort added, starting the engine.

'Yes, you're right. I wonder who it was.'

'Doesn't really matter, Mrs. F. Important thing is that the little girl is safe and sound. Comin' back to headquarters with me?'

'No, I have some errands to run. I'd appreciate it if you'd drop me off at Beth and Peter's floral shop.'

'Shall do.'

'And thanks for the coffee, Mort. It's getting better all the time.'

'Learned from the master,' he said, grinning.

*     *     *

The school auditorium was packed that night for the children's Halloween pageant. The production went smoothly, the only interruption coming when the same little boy who had to be excused from rehearsal to go to the restroom, expressed—loudly—the same request in the middle of the play, much to the delight of the audience.

After the show, I joined friends in the lobby, including flower shop owners Beth and Peter Mullin, the Lerners and Seth Hazlitt.

'Wasn't that adorable when the boy announced he had to go to the bathroom?' Joan said, laughing.

'Cute little fella,' Seth said.

Ed Lerner looked past me, and frowned. I turned to see what had caused his reaction. Lucas Tremaine stood at the other end of the lobby, talking with two women, one of whom I know, Brenda Brody. She works as copy editor at our monthly magazine, the *Cabot Cove Insider.*

Joan, too, saw Tremaine and wrapped her arms about herself. 'Gives me the creeps,' she said, 'having someone like that come to a children's pageant.'

'Show's open to the public,' Seth said.

'I know, I know,' said Joan, 'but there is something unsavory about him.'

My eyes went to the lobby's opposite corner, where Matilda Swift, dressed in her black duster and wearing her cat pendant, came from the auditorium, navigating knots of people, and was about to leave the school. Suddenly she stopped and cast a hard look in Tremaine's direction. I turned to him. He'd seen Matilda and glared back at her. Matilda's face was an angry mask; if her eyes were weapons, Tremaine would have been shot to death. She left the school, and Tremaine resumed his conversation with Brenda Brody and the other woman.

The feelings of apprehension I'd been experiencing lately, which I'd expressed to Matt Miller in my letter to him, returned. I suppose my face reflected it because Seth asked if I was feeling well.

'What?' I said.

'I asked if you were feeling all right.'

'Oh, yes, of course. I feel fine.'

We were joined by others and went out for coffee. I forced myself to take part in the easy banter, but couldn't shake the vague, free-floating anxiety that had taken over. The group broke up at eleven, and Seth dropped me at my house.

'Lookin' forward to tomorrow night?' he asked as I was about to get out of the car.

'Paul's party? Sure.'

'You don't look like you're in much of a party mood,' he said.

'Don't be silly. Paul's annual Halloween party is always fun. I can't wait.'

His skeptical expression said he didn't quite believe me, but he didn't press. I kissed his cheek. 'Thanks for the lift, Seth. See you tomorrow in all your military finery.'

## CHAPTER FIVE

'Seth, you look wonderful, so . . . so . . . so authentic.'

He beamed at the compliment on his costume from a party guest.

'Much obliged,' he said. 'I have Jessica to thank for it.'

'And you, Jessica, are absolutely scary. I can't believe you chose to come to the party as The Legend. What a great idea.'

'Thank you,' I said, not adding that I almost decided earlier that evening to abandon the getup and find a last-minute substitute.

It had taken me almost an hour to create the costume based upon the legend of Hepzibah Cabot. I wore a flowing white floor-length gauzy dress, and had gathered the ends of a long matching stole in front of me. I applied greenish white makeup that gave me the distinct look of a cadaver, and pulled on a long gray wig to which I'd attached strands of green crepe paper to achieve the effect of seaweed. The resulting image was, as my admirer later said, 'absolutely scary,' even to me when I looked in the mirror. My blue eyes deepened in intensity when contrasted with my now bleached skin, and the billowy white dress floated around my legs with each step I took, creating the impression of an ethereal figure not subject to gravity.

As I had studied my reflection, I'd experienced an overwhelming sense of apprehension. I put my hands up to cover the 'seaweed.' The woman looking back at me in the mirror bore a strong resemblance, I realized, to Matilda Swift.

An eerie feeling had again crept over me. I chided myself as I slipped my eye glasses into one pocket, and patted the other into which I'd tucked a comb and lipstick, as if they were talismans, reminders of who I really was. Fortunately, I didn't have time to dwell on macabre thoughts because the phone rang, startling me out of my doom-and-gloom funk.

'Jessica, it's Maureen,' Sheriff Metzger's wife said when I picked up the receiver.

'Hello, Maureen. Or should I call you Cher? All costumed up for the party?'

'Sure am. You?'

'I, ah . . . yes, I'm all set. Does Mort like the Revolutionary War costume he got from the theater?'

'He changed his mind. He's going as Davy Crockett instead. Marcia had this wonderful coonskin cap—not real fur, of course—and suede pants and shirt with fringe—just like the old TV show. Now he's complaining it makes him look fat.' She giggled. 'I think he's kind of cute in it. I'm just so grateful he won't be wearing his sheriff's uniform. I wanted to thank you for suggesting the theater costume department.'

'You're more than welcome. I'm sure you'll be the talk of the party. See you there.'

*       *       *

Paul Marshall viewed Halloween as a very special day to be celebrated. Other people treasured Thanksgiving as their favorite holiday, or Christmas, Hanukkah or Kwanza. But Marshall had always lavished special attention on the day of witches and goblins and other ghostly creatures.

It started, I'm told, when his wife died many years ago. Erica was just a little girl at the time, and her father felt a need to make up to her for the loss of her mother. While other holidays mean family celebrations, Halloween has long been an event for children—and grown-ups who enjoy dressing up like children, if only once a year. Paul made Halloween special for his daughter and her friends, and when she grew up, he continued the tradition of a Halloween party, now as much for himself as for her. His gardeners spent a week decorating the grounds, and the household staff devoted even more time and attention to turning the huge first-floor rooms of the main house into replicas of a vast dungeon, replete with catacombs and realistic spiderwebs, boiling cauldrons and faux stone walls. The sounds of rattling chains and eerie moans and cackles were piped through the stereo system, and grimacing jack-o'-lanterns and metal witch heads with pointed hats, flames dancing in their eyes from the illumination inside, were perched on every windowsill.

When I arrived with Seth at seven, the party had already begun. Catering and service trucks were parked on one side of the house, and the long driveway was lined with cars. Inside, about a hundred costumed citizens milled about to the strains of a Dixieland band. I'm not sure of the significance of Dixieland jazz to Halloween, but it didn't matter; the music was wonderful, two-beat and happy, causing toes to tap and heads to nod.

The costumes ran the gamut from inventive to mundane, outrageous to subdued. The most prevalent, of course, were the identical moose costumes worn by more than a dozen invited employees of Marshall-Scott Clothing, Inc. and members of the host's family. They were beautifully made, although I wondered how fatiguing—not to mention hot—it would be to carry the weight of those large moose heads all evening. Luckily for the moose people, it was a cool night.

There was no way of knowing whose faces were beneath the moose heads without talking to them, and even then I didn't recognize most of the voices. Paul Marshall, whose voice I did know, came to where I stood chatting with Seth Hazlitt, Mort and Maureen Metzger, and the town's newest lawyer, Joe Turco, and his date, who'd dressed as pilgrims. Like his employees, Paul wore a moose costume.

'My goodness, Mrs. Metzger, you do look just like Cher,' Marshall said to Maureen. 'Everyone looks wonderful.' His voice held a smile. When he is not wearing a bulky moose costume, Paul Marshall is a handsome man with a strong, square face, tanned complexion—either from a Caribbean vacation or a tanning salon—and expertly trimmed steel gray hair. Only his diminutive height saves him from the central-casting look of a chairman of the board. He is small, like his daughter, not as delicate of course, and compact. Nevertheless, he moves with the requisite ease of someone in control. He speaks in the pinched, nasal voice that mimics use to portray stereotypical old-money New England.

He and Tony Scott had made quite a financial success of Marshall-Scott Clothing, perhaps not quite a rags-to-riches story, but certainly a case of local boys making good. When his partner was alive; Paul used to kid that Tony was the brains and he, Paul, was the beauty, using his persuasive personality to build and market their business.

'Great night for a Halloween party, Mr. Marshall,' Maureen observed. 'The rain's stopped, and you've even got a full moon.'

'Please, we'll have no formality here this evening,' he said. 'It's Paul.' He turned to me. 'The Legend lives!'

'Only for one night,' I said.

'I think she's been living in one of my cottages ever since that dreadful woman arrived.'

'And who might that be?' Seth asked.

'The Swift woman, in the Rose Cottage,' Marshall replied. 'I've never paid any attention to whom the real estate broker rents the cottages to. She's never failed me before. But now . . . well, I think I'd better start paying more attention. All I know about Ms. Swift is what the agent told me, that she's from Massachusetts, has solid financial credentials, and claims to be an expert on roses. But she's been nothing but trouble. You heard, of course, about the Wandowski girl.'

'Yes,' I said. 'I was there. Really, it was just a misunderstanding. She was baking cookies and—'

We were interrupted by Warren Wilson, who removed his moose head to reveal a very pale damp brow, which he mopped with a white handkerchief.

'We were just discussing our tenant Ms.

Swift,' Marshall said. To me he added, 'Warren will be instituting eviction proceedings first thing next week.'

'Why?' I asked, not sure I should be debating what was obviously none of my business. 'Has she done anything to warrant that?'

Wilson answered the question. 'People in town are starting to talk about her, Mrs. Fletcher. She makes them uncomfortable. Paul doesn't want anyone on the property making trouble, and I agree with him a hundred percent. Everyone living on the property always got along just fine until she arrived. I haven't gone near the Rose Cottage since she moved in, she's so unpleasant.'

'But aren't you being unfair to her?' I started to say, but Marshall dismissed my comment with a wave of his arm, then excused himself and walked off, with Warren following close at his heels. The last words I heard were Marshall telling Wilson in gruff terms to put the moose head back on.

'Dance, Jessica?' Seth asked a few minutes later when the band began a slow version of 'Do You Know What It Means to Miss New Orleans?'

'Sure you want to dance with The Legend?' I asked playfully.

'Ghosts never harm physicians, Jessica.'

'Is that so?' I said, joining him on the dance floor with dozens of other couples. 'Physicians have special powers?'

'Of course. Every ghost knows that if they cross a medical doctor, they'll be banished to an HMO where they'll be denied necessary medical treatment by a clerk, and die a slow, painful death.'

I smiled and changed the subject. Give Seth Hazlitt, M.D., an excuse to complain about the current state of medicine, and he makes good use of it.

The song had almost ended, and Seth was in the process of leading me into a death-defying old-fashioned dip, when I started to laugh.

'I know I'm not Fred Astaire,' he said, but—'

'No, no,' I said, 'it isn't you. Look over there.'

He followed my gaze to where two moose were dancing slowly to the song's rhythm, their huge moose heads snuggled against each other. One was considerably taller than the other and had to bend down for their cheeks to touch.

'I hope someone is taking pictures,' I said, still watching the furry couple.

'Richard is.'

Richard Koser, Cabot Cove's preeminent photographer, moved close to the swaying couple and took a few shots.

'I wonder who they are,' I said as we left the dance floor, thinking that the shorter moose might be Erica Marshall.

'Can't hardly tell,' Seth said, leading me to

67

one of three portable bars, where he ordered two glasses of an orange-colored punch created by the bartenders for the occasion. The taste of pumpkin juice was unmistakable.

'Great party, huh?' said Doug Treyz, reaching for two glasses of punch. Doug, my dentist, wore a 1920s golfing outfit; his wife, Tina, was costumed as Marie Antoinette, or some other lady of the eighteenth century.

'Wonderful, as usual,' I said.

We were joined by Joan and Ed Lerner, and Jack and Marilou Decker, publishers of the *Cabot Cove Insider*, the award-winning monthly magazine that chronicles the comings and goings of our citizens.

'I never want to see another moose, unless it's the real thing,' Jack quipped. He flipped up the black eye patch of his pirate costume and plucked two hors d'oeuvres from a passing tray held by a very pretty witch. After popping one of the hors d'oeuvres into his mouth, he handed the other to his wife, who wore a matching outfit.

'I keep trying to tell the female moose from the male moose,' Marilou said, 'but those details seem to have been left out by the costume designer.'

Ed Lerner was dressed as a grizzly bear. 'Bear is his nickname,' explained Joan, who wore a University of Michigan cheerleader costume. 'Oh, by the way, Ed and I have decided to have a Veteran's Day party in

November. Everyone has to dress military. You'll be perfect in that uniform, Dr. Hazlitt.'

The Lerners drifted off, and the rest of our little group eventually gravitated from the main room to one of several patios overlooking the sprawling grounds of the Marshall estate. Rain earlier in the day had emptied the clouds, and it was now a cool, clear night, the chill a welcome contrast to the party inside, where it had become increasingly warm.

'You'd never know Paul Marshall was in financial difficulty, judging from this place,' Doug Treyz said absently.

'Is he?' Decker asked.

'That's the scuttlebutt from my treatment chair,' the dentist said. 'The way I hear it, his partner, Scott, never did come up with a solution for BarrierCloth's flamability problem, and paid the price with his life. Without that, the company can't compete with L. L. Bean and Lands' End.'

'One of my patients told me that the two partners took out hefty "key man" insurance policies not long before the accident,' Seth said. 'Paul should have collected on the policy—millions, I understand.'

'Yes, but I heard the company hasn't paid yet because of the suspicious nature of the fire,' Tina Treyz added.

'Looks like if you want to know anyone's financial condition around here, go for a root

69

canal or a routine physical,' Marilou said, raising her eyebrows.

'Maybe he did perfect the formula,' Decker offered. 'I heard he might have.'

A pair of large white doves, or maybe they were swans, joined us on the patio. They turned out to be Peter and Roberta Walters, owners of the area's only radio station. 'These people keep up on the news,' Jack Decker said, turning to the new couple. 'We were just speculating on whether Tony Scott solved the flame problem with BarrierCloth before he died.'

'Can't prove it by me,' Pete Walters said. 'What's new with the nut out on the old quarry road?'

'Lucas Tremaine?' Decker said. 'Our copy editor, Brenda Brody, has been attending his . . . what would you call them, services?'

'Con games,' Seth said, guffawing.

'She calls them seances,' Marilou interjected. 'You know Brenda lost her husband a year ago.'

'Ayuh,' said Seth. 'He was my patient. Fell off a ladder while putting on a new roof. Damn fool was too old to be roofing.'

'Brenda believes in reincarnation and the ability to speak to the dead. I told her that giving money to Tremaine was a waste, but when someone is grieving the way she is, you grasp at straws. She swears Tremaine puts her in touch with Russell, that they have long conversations.'

'The man is a charlatan,' Doug said.

'Unconscionable,' added Pete.

'There's got to be a law against what he's doing,' Seth said.

'If there were,' I put in, 'Mort Metzger would have invoked it long ago.'

'Look at that.'

We directed our eyes to the right, where Tina Treyz was pointing. Two party-goers in moose costumes could be seen walking through the small, ancient cemetery adjacent to Marshall's property, where The Legend and her unfaithful spouse were buried. The moose couple's antlered heads were silhouettes in the light of the full moon. Beyond the cemetery, I knew, were two cottages, the Rose Cottage, where Matilda Swift lived, and on the other side of a grove of spruce trees, the one inhabited by Robert and Lauren Wandowski and their daughter.

'Sneaking off for a little moose smooching, I suspect,' Seth said, smiling.

I turned to my right, where a lonely figure in a moose costume stood on a second patio, gazing out over the cemetery, where the couple was walking. Although he or she was a considerable distance from me, I could see from the stiff stance and fisted gloves that this person was not happy. Seconds later, another moose joined the first. The two exchanged a few words before stepping from view.

'That music is too good to waste,' Roberta Walters said, swinging her tail feathers around and taking her husband's wing. 'You promised me two dances this evening. You owe me one.'

We followed the Walters inside and wandered through the elaborate decorations in Paul Marshall's mansion. In the dining room, where the walls and chandelier were draped with cotton cobwebs, a buffet rivaling the best on any cruise ship was set up along one wall. Cold shrimp and oysters cascading over tiered ice sculptures were displayed next to pots of hot chowder, pastas, carving stations of turkey, roast beef and lamb, and more salads and side dishes than I'd have time, or stomach, to sample.

Across from the buffet was a table right out of Dickens's *Great Expectations*. It had been set to re-create Miss Havisham's long-abandoned banquet platters of moldy food, dusty champagne glasses tipped over and skeins of cobwebs on the candelabra that tilted in its center. Guests had gathered to admire the culinary displays both real and counterfeit, but before we were invited to partake of the overflowing buffet tables, our host asked that we gather around him at the foot of a winding staircase leading up to the second floor.

'Ladies and gentlemen, my dear friends, I am so happy to see all of you here enjoying yourselves, and I know you'll continue the festivities at the buffet tables. But it would be derelict of me not to mention that this night marks the one-year anniversary of the untimely, tragic death of a man who was not only my trusted partner, but also my friend. I speak, of course, of Anthony Scott, who died in that terrible fire one year ago today. Would you join me in a moment of silent tribute to his memory?'

Marshall lowered his head, and a hush fell over the room. Then he looked out over the throng of revelers, raised a glass of champagne he'd been holding and said, 'To Tony Scott, partner, genius and sorely missed friend.'

Those holding drinks answered by raising their glasses.

'Tony was a shy man, but he loved a good party, so I know he'd want you to enjoy this one. Now, get to those buffet tables,' Marshall sang out. 'Bon appetit!'

The adage that time passes when you're having fun certainly applied to this particular evening and party, and I couldn't believe how quickly the night slipped by. Before I knew it, waiters and waitresses were bringing in trays of magnificent desserts specially baked for the party by one of Boston's top bakeries, many of the sweets decorated with imaginative Halloween figures, tiny marzipan witches and pumpkins and white chocolate ghosts and other symbols identified with the day.

By midnight, most of the guests, filled with food and conviviality, had said good night to their host and gotten into cars delivered to the front portico by parking attendants hired for the occasion. Before the guests left, however, the women were each presented with a small sterling silver paperweight in the shape of a pumpkin, the men a silver tie clasp formed to resemble a broomstick, mementos of a memorable evening.

'Shall we, Jessica?' Seth asked me a half hour later.

We'd lingered to chat with the Metzgers and the Lerners.

'I'm ready,' I said. 'I can't wait to shed The Legend and get back to being just Jessica.'

'Me, too,' Maureen said. 'It was fun being Cher for a night, but I wouldn't want to have to dress up like this every day.'

'Well, you can come as you normally are to our party,' Joan said with a smile, 'providing you wear something slightly military.'

As we started for the door, Paul Marshall approached. 'Not leaving so soon, are you?' he said.

'So soon?' Seth said. 'Long past my bedtime.'

'Oh, stay a few minutes longer,' Paul said. 'I've asked a special few to join me for a nightcap. You'll hurt my feelings if you go.'

As much as I wanted to leave, it would have been impolite, I felt, to decline his invitation. Paul told a waiter to deliver a tray of brandy to the living room, and Seth and I, along with the

Metzgers and Lerners, followed him there, where a small group, many in moose costumes, mingled. The patio doors were open, and guests wandered in and out. A skeleton staff—literally since that's how they were costumed—had begun to gather the dishes and glassware and other remains of the party, and to bring back the furniture that had been removed to make room for the dance floor. Marshall grabbed one of the moose. 'Have you seen Erica?'

The moose shook his head, and Paul sent him—I think it was a him—to turn off the sound effects, which were still groaning and rattling in the background.

'Please excuse me. I won't be but a moment,' our host said. 'A little business to take care of.' He strode from the room.

As the Metzgers and the Lerners went to join the Deckers on the patio, Seth looked at me and shrugged. 'Might as well sit down,' he said. 'Bein' on my feet for so long's got me all tuckered out.' He moved toward a wing chair, one of a pair flanking a marble fireplace, and sank into its soft cushion with a grateful sigh. I took the chair opposite and watched as one of the skeletons made the rounds of the room, delivering drink orders.

Marshall rejoined us several minutes later and pulled up a chair. His voice was hearty, the success of the party obviously buoying his spirits.

'You know, I never get a chance to really talk with my guests,' he said. 'There are so many things that pull me away during the evening.'

'It was a wonderful Halloween party, Paul— as usual,' I said as the waiter appeared with brandy in snifters. 'Thank you for inviting us.'

'Thank you for coming. Wouldn't be as much fun without you. By the way, you look terrific as The Legend. Are you sure I didn't just see you haunting the cemetery?'

'This is the night she's supposed to appear,' Seth put in, 'but I can vouch for Jessica's presence all evening.'

Paul started to say something, but changed his mind and said instead, 'Yes, tonight was fun. I just wish Tony could have been here to share in it.'

'Yes, I'm sure you do,' I said. I tasted the brandy, then put the glass down. The natural heat felt good going down, but I was tired and knew the drink would make me more so.

'We were like brothers,' Marshall said, waving the waiter away, 'much more than business partners. I just can't accept that he's no longer here. When I first learned he'd died in that explosion and fire in his lab, I—'

A loud wail cut through the air. All conversation stopped, and the small cluster of guests looked up.

'I thought I told you to turn off the sound,' Marshall growled at a nearby moose.

'I did,' the masculine voice responded.

The wail erupted again, raising the fine hairs on my arms. We jumped up as a group and rushed onto the patio, where we peered out over the dark property in the direction from which the sound seemed to have come. We heard it again, louder this time, now closer to a scream, coming from the cemetery, or beyond.

'Good Lord,' Paul said.

'I'd better see what's happening,' Mort said, instantly shifting into his law enforcement mode.

He took off at a run, the rest of us following. We raced to the cemetery, the damp earth pulling at our shoes. Dodging tombstones and grave markers—nothing there—we continued running downhill toward the Rose Cottage. The screams had stopped by now, but we followed the sound of sobbing. As we approached, two figures could be seen standing together near the bare branches of rose bushes that climbed the brick wall. The two people were in costume, their bodies so close together their moose heads touched.

'Stand back!' Mort ordered, bringing us to a halt. We weren't so far away that we couldn't see what had caught his attention. There, in a pool of moonlight, lay a motionless form. A stain, the same rich hue as the roses that bloomed on this brick wall every spring, had turned white hair to crimson. Those incredibly blue eyes were open and dull. It was Matilda Swift.

## CHAPTER SIX

Sheriff Mort Metzger, dressed in his Davy Crockett costume, stretched his arms out wide and stopped the forward motion of the small crowd. 'Come on, folks, give us a little room, huh. Dr. Hazlitt, would you . . .?'

Seth walked to the recumbent figure and slowly, with obvious arthritic stiffness, lowered himself to one knee so he could place his fingertips against Matilda's neck.

'Is she dead?' Mort asked, pulling his badge from a back pocket and pinning it above the suede fringe on his shirt.

'Ayuh. Looks like it,' Seth replied, his fingers now on the chin of the corpse, gently moving it back and forth to check, I knew, whether rigor mortis had begun to set in. Witnessing this macabre tableau, besides Seth, Mort and me, were a movie star, a pair of pirates, two swans, a bear, a cheerleader and a half dozen moose. Had it not been so real and tragic, it might have been a surrealistic scene from a Fellini movie.

'Who could have done such a thing?' Paul Marshall's voice boomed as he pushed his way to the front of the group and tugged off his costume head.

Mort turned from the corpse and faced us. 'First thing, everybody get rid a' those damn moose heads so I can see who I'm talking to.'

One by one, the guests pulled off their furry heads until their identities were exposed.

'Who discovered the body?' Mort asked, turning to the couple who'd been there when we arrived at the scene. 'Who screamed?'

'I did,' replied Erica Marshall, dropping her animal head to the ground.

'Erica!' Warren Wilson's face was red as he flung his moose head to the side and glared across the body at her. 'I've been looking all over for you.'

'What were you doing down here?' her father asked in a tone that demanded an answer.

'I was . . . I was taking a walk, getting some air,' she said.

Marshall turned to the moose standing next to her. 'You,' he growled, 'do as the sheriff said. Take off that head!'

Jeremy Scott slowly removed his costume head and dropped it next to Erica's.

'You were here with Erica?' Wilson said, the anger in his voice rivaling Marshall's.

When Jeremy didn't respond, Erica's father repeated the question.

'No, sir,' Jeremy said nervously. 'I just got here, a few seconds before—'

'Hey, you there,' Mort interrupted as he

spotted a moose standing behind Jack Decker's broad pirate hat. 'Take off your head right now.'

The tall figure hesitated, but with all eyes upon him, he realized he didn't have any choice except to follow the order. He reluctantly pulled on his snout until the head slid off, revealing Robert Wandowski. His face was pale, and his dark hair stood on end from static electricity. 'I . . . I . . . I didn't do anything,' he stammered. 'I swear I didn't. Even though I didn't like her, after she lured my daughter into her house—'

'Just calm down,' Mort said, 'and be quiet. And don't leave until we get your statement.'

'I will, Sheriff. I'll stand right here.'

I wondered where Wandowski's wife was. Mort patted his back pocket. 'I got my beeper, but the phone's in the car.' He took in the group. 'Somebody call nine-one-one,' he said. 'Tell 'em we've got a dead body on the Paul Marshall estate and to send my deputies and an EMS team on the double. And rustle up the ME.'

Jeremy started for the front door of the cottage.

'Where are you going?' Mort demanded.

'To call nine-one-one,' Jeremy replied.

'Not in there, you don't. That's part of the crime scene. Go up to the house.'

'How did you know there's a phone in there?' Jack Decker asked Jeremy.

Jeremy held up his hands in a gesture of bewilderment. 'I just assumed there's one,' he replied nervously, taking off at a run up to the main house.

'Stay away from the cottage,' Mort told us. 'I don't want any more footprints added to the scene here.'

Mort was right not to allow anyone into the cottage without police supervision. It was always possible that some piece of evidence might be inadvertently compromised or tainted, including the phone.

I shifted my position to try to see through the open door into the cottage, but my attention was directed back to Mort, who was addressing the crowd. A few curious people had begun to inch closer to the body. While some averted their eyes from viewing it directly, like watching a gory scene in a motion picture through slightly spread fingers, others faced it head-on, moving in for a better look. Since, to my knowledge, none of them knew the deceased well, the shock that energized the crowd was the result of a murder having been committed, not the loss of someone they cared about.

'Get back,' Mort shouted, directing the group away from the body. He turned to Erica. 'You see anybody down here, Ms. Marshall?'

'No! I mean, no one but . . . her.' She pointed at the body and turned away, the fingers of her right hand hovering in front of

81

her mouth, her eyes still wide with fear.

'Anybody see anything unusual tonight?' Mort asked.

'Why are you asking us, Sheriff?' Paul Marshall demanded. 'This was obviously the work of a madman who strayed onto the property. Surely, you don't think anyone invited to my party might have killed her.'

Mort ignored Marshall and faced Seth, who remained on his knees; I didn't know whether he'd stayed there next to the body because he was still examining it or was having trouble getting up. Mort knelt at his side. 'Well, Doc, what do you think?' he asked loud enough for us to hear.

'Somebody hit her pretty hard,' Seth said, adjusting his position to better see where she'd been struck in the head.

'What sort a' weapon?' Mort asked.

'Hard to say,' Seth replied, continuing to scrutinize Matilda. 'I'm no medical examiner, but it was a pretty large object, something flat.'

Mort stood. 'Anybody see anything around here could've been the weapon?' He extended his hand to assist Seth to his feet.

As onlookers swiveled in search of a possible weapon, Joan Lerner dropped to her knees. 'Here, kitty, kitty,' she called softly.

A large black cat, back arched, was rubbing its side against the corner of the cottage. Large yellow eyes gazed warily at the intruders in its domain.

'Ah, the witch's familiar,' Peter Walters muttered. 'The spirit that accompanies her everywhere.'

His wife swatted his arm. 'Peter, you're as bad as those people in town. This is no time to kid.'

As Joan moved slowly toward the cat, it gave out with a yowl, quickly turned around, tail high, and disappeared behind a hedge.

'We can't just leave the cat.' Joan frowned, brushing mud off her hands. 'There's no one here now to feed it.'

I didn't mention that cats are natural hunters and that this one looked like it could easily find prey. Instead, I said, 'I'll call Artie Sack later. He's the gardener who lives on the estate. I'm sure he'll be glad to care for the cat. He's always over here pruning and watering the rose bushes. In fact, he's right over there.' I pointed to where Jeremy, followed by Artie, trotted back from the Marshall mansion.

'Good, Jessica,' Joan said. 'I would have worried.'

Jeremy Scott went straight to Mort. 'I had some trouble getting through,' he panted, out of breath. 'The line was full of static. Artie here found me a phone that worked. They're on their way.'

Artie blushed at what he perceived as a compliment. He looked down and shuffled his feet, then saw the body and cringed. A moan escaped his lips. He squeezed his eyes shut and began rocking back and forth, hugging his shoulders and making mewling sounds. Mort put his arm around him and turned him away from the body. 'It's okay, Artie,' he said, 'nothing to do with you. Go on home. You've already helped enough.'

A few minutes later, flashing lights were seen in the circular driveway of the Marshall home, and we were joined by two of Mort's uniformed deputies, one with a camera dangling around his neck and carrying a heavy box, the other holding a small black bag from which he pulled a roll of yellow crime scene tape. They were followed by a pair of white-coated EMS technicians toting a stretcher, and the county's medical examiner, Alfred Gillo, who'd been appointed to that post only six months earlier.

'Where's Harold?' Mort shouted at one of the deputies.

'I got hold of him, Sheriff, and filled him in. He should be here soon.'

'Where was he?'

'Down the quarry road, helping a motorist with a flat. You know how rough that road is.'

'What about the state guys, Jerry? We're gonna need security help overnight, and crime scene personnel.'

'Called them, too. Should be a couple 'a cars here soon.'

Jerry put down his heavy load, which, it turned out, contained a battery pack and lights. He set up the lights and plugged in the cords, then pressed a switch. A brilliant white light instantly flooded the scene, demarcating everything in its path from pebbles in the mud to the now-crusting blood in Matilda's hair, and casting deep shadows where its illumination failed to reach. The front of the Rose Cottage lit up like the scrim for a fashion magazine photo shoot.

'Don't think we need to tent the scene, Sheriff,' Jerry said. 'Not fixing to rain again tonight.'

Squinting against the sudden brightness, Mort nodded and started barking instructions, ordering our group to move farther away from the lighted area so the officers had room to work.

'Jerry, take your photos so these guys can continue doin' their job,' he said, pointing to the EMS crew.

'Right, Sheriff.'

'Wendell, get out the spray paint so you can mark the position of the body when Jerry's finished takin' pictures.'

'Yes, sir. Right away, sir. I mean, as soon as Jerry's done, sir.'

Wendell Watson was a rookie who'd recently joined the force. He'd whet his appetite for police work after serving as my security escort when I was in New York City for the opening of a play on Broadway, *Knock 'Em Dead*, based upon one of my books.

Following some unsettling incidents there, including the murder of the play's producer, Mort insisted I have a bodyguard and sent Wendell to protect me. He was persistent, if not exactly skilled, and I'm still not sure who protected whom, but everything turned out all right. Wendell returned to Cabot Cove full of enthusiasm for life as a peace officer and enrolled in the next available class at the Maine Police Academy. Once he became one of Mort's deputies, he was paired with Jerry, an experienced officer, to ensure that he could continue to learn his chosen profession—and not make too many mistakes in the process.

'Jerry, I want photos of the cottage, too, inside and out. Did you get the body and all around here?'

'I did, Sheriff, although there's already been a lot of tramplin' on the scene.'

'Couldn't be helped.' Mort turned to Wendell. 'Wendell, stop pacin' like that. You're just addin' your footprints to the others.'

'Yes, sir.'

Wendell gave the can of spray paint a vigorous shake and carefully traced the outline of Matilda's body, his Adam's apple bobbing up and down as he swallowed compulsively when his arm neared her bloody head. When he'd completed the task, he stepped away, and the EMS crew and medical examiner took over.

Wearing latex gloves, both to protect themselves and to keep from contaminating evidence, the two technicians first confirmed what had been evident, that Matilda was dead. They then placed plastic bags over her hands and secured the bags with rubber bands to keep them from falling off. Mort knelt beside them to check her clothing for pockets. His mouth a grim line, he gingerly rocked the body from one side to the other, searching for evidence. He removed items from her person and dropped them into separate clear plastic bags, which he handed to Wendell. Directed by the medical examiner, the EMS crew laid out a black body bag alongside the corpse and gently lifted Matilda's body into the rubber cocoon. One tucked in her skirt and collar while the other zipped the bag closed. It never failed to impress me, the respectful way emergency technicians deal with the dead. Matilda was certainly unknown to them, yet they treated her remains as if she were a cherished friend or family member. I hoped she was someone's cherished family member, and didn't envy Mort the responsibility of imparting the sad news.

When the ambulance drove off, the group that had stayed after the party began to get restless.

'How long are you going to keep us here, Sheriff?' Paul asked. 'My guests are falling asleep on their feet.'

'I know you're all tired, Mr. Marshall, but if you'll bear with us a few more minutes, we'll get everyone's name and where you were all evening, then let you go home.'

I drew Mort aside and spoke quietly into his ear. 'Mort, why not let Paul bring everyone back to the house so they can at least sit down? We can wait there until you finish your preliminary work and can join us.'

'Good idea, Mrs. F.' To Wendell he said, 'Escort these folks up to Mr. Marshall's house and stay with them. I'll be there as soon as Jerry and I finish up down here.'

Wendell hesitated, a look of disappointment on his freckled young face. He obviously wanted to stay at Mort's side at the crime scene.

'Go on, Wendell, start by takin' names, addresses and phone numbers,' Mort said while helping Jerry unroll a long ribbon of yellow plastic with CRIME SCENE—DO NOT CROSS repeated every foot along its length.

Wendell immediately brightened. He hitched up his belt and turned to the weary revelers. 'C'mon, ladies and gentlemen, we'll walk back to the house now. Stay close together, please. I don't want to lose anybody.'

Joan cleared her throat. 'Officer,' she said.

'Yes, ma'am?'

'I think you might already have lost one.'

'What do you mean, ma'am?'

'Well, there were six moose when we first

got here. Now there are five.'

'You sure about that, Mrs. Lerner?' Mort asked.

'Yes, very sure. I counted them right after we came down here. Why, I don't know, but I did.'

'She's right,' I added. 'There were six moose when we first arrived on the scene. I counted them, too.'

Everyone's attention turned to the brown, furry forms and silently counted. Present and accounted for were Paul and Erica Marshall, Warren Wilson, Jeremy Scott and Robert Wandowski.

Mort, who'd begun securing the tape to a branch of one of the multiple rose bushes lining the drive, looked up at the house as another squad car came to a screeching halt, its headlights bouncing off the residence's brick walls. The distraction caused him to catch a thorn on the back of his finger. He mumbled and dropped the spool of yellow tape to the ground, jamming the bleeding knuckle into his mouth. He waited as another of his deputies, Harold Jenkins, came down the path in our direction. He wasn't alone. A figure walked in front of him. As they approached, I saw that the person with Harold was wearing a moose costume identical to those worn by the others. Handcuffs securing the new arrival's hands in front made it clear that this was a moose in custody.

'What've we got here?' Mort asked.

Harold grinned. 'Ran across this moose on my way here, Sheriff. Found him climbing over that fence at the end of the property, up by the quarry road.'

Our sixth moose, I thought. Who was inside that heavy, furry costume, and why had he run from the scene? I assumed it was a man because the person in the costume was fairly tall.

Mort approached the newcomer and said, 'Take off that head.' When he didn't comply, Mort ordered him to lean forward. With a push from Harold, the moose bent from the waist but kept his head stiff. Mort grabbed the two antlers and pulled. The hair on the bowed head was long and drawn back into a ponytail. He straightened, his posture erect, his eyes challenging.

'Good evening ladies and gentlemen,' a smiling Lucas Tremaine said.

## CHAPTER SEVEN

The Marshall manor house was in the process of being put back to its usual elegant decor when the remnants of the party guests trudged in and collapsed on silk brocade chairs and sofas arranged in conversation groups around the living room. The furniture that had been removed for the party was again in place, but the cobwebs, cauldrons, faux stone walls and many decorations that had given the mansion its eerie Halloween atmosphere had yet to be removed. It seemed as if we'd stumbled into a movie studio where the set for a horror film was being cleared to make room for a Regency drama. A diligent crew loaded tables and chairs into huge moving trucks outside; the caterer had departed earlier, taking trays of leftovers, I later learned, to drop off at a shelter for teenage runaways down the coast. Apart from the trucks and patrol cars, the few vehicles remaining in the driveway belonged to those of us still at the house.

Harold Jenkins led Lucas Tremaine to the center of the room and pressed him into an empty fan-back chair.

'I want these handcuffs removed,' Tremaine demanded.

Harold appeared unsure of what to do.

'I haven't broken any laws,' Tremaine said. 'You have no right to shackle me like some common criminal. Take them off!'

'Mr. Tremaine, if I remove your handcuffs, do I have your word you'll stay right here till the sheriff says you can go?'

Tremaine cocked his head, a smirk on his lips. 'You have my word as a gentleman. I am at your service, Officer. Actually, I rather like this house. I'll stay until—' He looked to where Paul Marshall sat and added, 'Until our gracious host asks me to leave.'

That brought Paul out of his chair. He charged across the room and stood directly in front of Tremaine, looking down at him. 'I want to know what you're doing here. How did you get one of my moose costumes and crash the party?'

Harold inserted himself between the men. 'Let's just take it easy, Mr. Marshall,' he said. 'I'm sure we'll find out all about that once the sheriff gets back. Please sit down.'

As Marshall returned to his seat and Harold unlocked Tremaine's cuffs, Ed Lerner said to Peter Walters, 'That's the crackpot who's always giving speeches in the village about ghosts and goblins. Joan and I told the sheriff just the other day about overhearing folks threatening to chase him out of town.'

'He's the one,' Walters agreed. 'Do you know why he was cuffed? Is he the prime suspect in the murder?'

'I don't know.'

'I should get to the radio station,' Walters said. 'This is a big story. I need a pad and pen. Better yet, a tape recorder.'

Walters's wife, Roberta, turned to her husband. 'Peter,' she said, 'you're molting all over the floor.' Half the feathers from his elbows and knees had fallen off his bird costume to the carpet.

'Do you think they'll let me use the phone?' Walters asked no one in particular as he stood and started to cross the large room. Harold politely asked him to remain seated until Mort arrived.

'Look,' Walters told the deputy, 'you know me. I own the radio station. People will start hearing rumors about this and go off half-cocked. I'm a journalist. It's always the best thing to report a story as fast as possible and get the facts out.'

'Yes, sir, Mr. Walters, I know who you are, but—'

Walters exhibited a rare anger. 'Ever hear of the First Amendment?' he snapped.

'Yes, sir,' Harold replied, 'but it seems to me murder is a little more important right about now. Please, Mr. Walters, don't make my job any tougher.'

Walters sighed and returned to his seat next to his wife, who, it seemed to me, was struggling to stay awake, a condition many of us shared.

When we'd raced to the Rose Cottage in response to Erica Marshall's screams and found Matilda Swift's body, the air had been charged with energy. The shock of the murder had adrenaline pouring into our veins, reversing the normal lassitude after an evening of eating, drinking and dancing. But now that the initial excitement had ebbed, a pervasive fatigue set in. I looked around the room and hoped Mort would return quickly. His witnesses, at least those of us still there, were fading fast.

People were slumped in their chairs, staring at one another with blank expressions. Seth had found the same wing chair in front of the fireplace he'd occupied earlier and fought to keep his chin from lowering to his chest. Marilou Decker rested her head on her husband's shoulder. Joan Lerner, in her cheerleader uniform, and Mort's wife, Maureen, dressed up like Cher, resembled oddly mismatched bookends, camped out as they were on either end of a blue moiré sofa, each woman leaning back, head angled toward an upholstered arm. It had been a long night, and it surely wasn't over.

Paul sat at the end of a line of moose. He looked shell-shocked. His exhausted daughter was flanked by two scowling young men, Jeremy and Warren, whose animosity toward each other was palpable. Aside from Harold, who was hovering over Lucas Tremaine, and Wendell, who was standing next to the patio doors, only an agitated Robert Wandowski was still on his feet, pacing back and forth in a corner, reminding me more of a caged Colorado mountain lion than a docile Maine moose.

Mort entered the room and rapped his knuckles on a French writing table to draw everyone's attention. He'd taken off his Davy Crockett hat but was still clad in the buckskin shirt and pants. 'Ladies and gentlemen, we're

94

all tired, I know,' he said, 'but Wendell here is going to take down some information while I finish up at the Rose Cottage. After I talk to each of you briefly, you'll be free to go home. I caution you not to leave town. We'll probably be interviewing all of you again in the next couple 'a days.'

It struck me as I sat in a chair near Seth that those gathered in the room were the most unlikely of suspects in a murder, but I also knew that Mort had a job to do and would go by the book.

'Sheriff, Mr. Marshall and I were scheduled to be away a few days on business,' Warren said, shooting Jeremy a smug look.

'Sorry, gentlemen, but I'm afraid you'll have to postpone that trip for a while.'

Jeremy sat back and smiled. Warren, face scarlet, busied himself polishing the lenses of his glasses on his furry sleeve.

'This is just ridiculous,' Marshall grumbled. 'Go question those cleaning people outside. My guests are not murderers, except maybe that one, who by the way certainly was not invited into this house.' He pointed at Tremaine. 'I can't put my business on hold, Sheriff, while you play cops-and-robbers. Why don't you get some experts in here who know how to conduct a murder investigation?'

'Daddy, please, you're not helping things,' Erica said.

'Don't you talk to me in that tone, young

lady. I'll—'

'Mr. Marshall,' Mort interrupted smoothly, ignoring the insulting comment, 'I'll need your guest list. Do you have a copy handy?'

'No. Alice, my secretary, handled the invitations. She went home an hour ago.'

'Well, I'd be real appreciative if you'd give her a call and have her run that list over to the office first thing tomorrow morning. And maybe Miss Marshall would be kind enough to make some coffee, if it wouldn't be too much bother.'

'It's no bother at all, Sheriff.' Erica stood, obviously relieved to get away from her unpleasant companions.

'I'll be just another fifteen minutes or so,' Mort said. 'Wendell, start taking down IDs.' He swung open the patio doors and disappeared past them.

'Erica,' I said, 'I'll give you a hand with the coffee.'

'I'll help you, Erica,' Warren said, jumping to his feet. Jeremy grabbed his sleeve. 'Mrs. Fletcher is already helping her,' he said. 'They don't need you.'

'Who do you thinking you're talking to, Scott? I'm not one of your marketing flunkies.' He wrenched his arm from Jeremy's grasp.

'No, you just think you can get ahead by romancing the boss's daughter.'

'Cut it out, both of you!' Paul ordered.

Erica and I walked down a hall to the rear

of the house. 'Everyone's tired,' I said, trying not to sound as though I was, too. 'Jeremy and Warren will get over it once they've gotten some sleep.'

'I doubt that, Mrs. Fletcher. They hate each other. Ever since Jeremy learned that Warren and I have been dating, he's been very cold to me.'

'Jealous?'

'If he is, it's only because he's ambitious, too. They don't care about me, either of them. It's all business. Jeremy came here from California to make sure no one steals his father's formula. He wants the patent and the royalties.'

The cold, matter-of-fact way in which she delivered her analysis of the situation took me aback for a moment. Surely, I thought, the motives of both Jeremy and Warren couldn't be that calculating. Had this pretty young woman become so jaded, so cynical, that she was incapable of accepting affection from men who were interested in her? If that was the case, had her relationship with her father been so strained that it had led her to this hardened view of life? It was clear from things she'd said earlier that she and her father did not enjoy the most cordial of parent-sibling relationships. What was behind that? I wondered. Was Paul Marshall so domineering that he'd stripped his daughter of her ability to love? I hoped not.

Erica pushed open a swinging door leading

97

into a huge kitchen. Unlike the formal room we'd just left, the atmosphere in this one was cheery and comfortable with tile floors from the local quarry, hanging plants in front of tall windows, fruitwood cabinets and modern stainless steel appliances. A long country table that served as a work space held clean trays, bowls and utensils from the evening's buffet.

At one end of the room a curved extension lined with windows jutted out into the garden. Inside it, a round table was covered with a pale yellow linen cloth and set for breakfast for three. I remembered that Jeremy was a house guest, and thought the tension between the young people must make for some uncomfortable meals.

'I was hoping there was some leftover coffee from the party, but they must have thrown it out already,' Erica said. She crossed to a large coffee urn on a sideboard near the alcove and lifted the lid. 'Oh, look, it's already set up for tomorrow. That's a bit of luck.' She flipped the switch. 'We told the staff they didn't have to come back till noon tomorrow to finish the clean-up. Mrs. Sack must have done this. She's Artie's sister-in-law. Do you know Artie?'

'Oh, yes, a nice man and a wonderful gardener. He does work for me, too.'

'I keep forgetting that Artie works for others in the village. Anyway, Mrs. Sack is our housekeeper, and she always sets up the morning coffee in the evening before she leaves. It looks like she made extra in case we had guests. Should be plenty.'

Erica sighed as she sank into one of a quartet of wicker chairs surrounding the small, table. 'Please, Mrs. Fletcher, sit down. You must be tired, too.'

'I am, but the aroma of the coffee is already waking me up. Shall we get the cups ready, and milk and sugar?'

'In a minute. I don't think I can lift my arms right now.'

'Point out where everything is and I'll get what we need.'

'Just sit for a minute,' she said, a small, weary smile crossing her pretty face. 'Please. We'll do it together once the coffee's brewed.'

I took the chair closest to her.

'What an awful evening,' she said.

'Did you know Matilda Swift very well?' I asked.

'I didn't know her at all. She moved here several months ago after the cottage was redone. My father fixed it up after Tony died. He gutted the whole place, and then had a decorator come in to furnish it. That's when the magazine people did the story on the rose garden.'

'You must have spoken with her at some point,' I said, not wanting to sound as though I was prying. 'She was your neighbor.'

'Not really. A nodding acquaintance at most. She kept to herself. Tell me, Mrs.

Fletcher, have you lived in Cabot Cove all your life?'

'It certainly feels that way,' I said, 'although there was a time when I was still teaching that I moved down south.' I laughed. 'Massachusetts. "Down south" as Mara at the luncheonette would say.'

'Were you away long?'

'I taught there for several years, but when I met my husband, Frank, he was eager to move to Cabot Cove. I'd told him so many stories about how wonderful my hometown was, he wanted to see if it could possibly be as idyllic as my descriptions. But we were talking about Matilda.'

'The only time I ever lived away from home was during college, but that was only as far as Connecticut.'

'Well, you're young yet. About Matilda—'

Erica rushed on as if she hadn't heard me. 'My mother's family came from there, but I really haven't had much contact with them. I think they didn't like my father, and when my mother died—I was just a baby—they didn't bother to keep in touch.' She twisted sideways in her chair so she could prop her arm on its back and rest her chin in her hand.

'I only met your mother once, I believe,' I said. 'A lovely woman.'

'I don't remember her at all. When I was little, Jeremy's mother was like family to me, but then she moved away, taking Jeremy, and I never saw her again.'

'It must have been difficult for your father, as a single man, raising you alone. He's done a wonderful job.'

'Well, he always had plenty of help,' Erica said, her voice suddenly hard. 'Mrs. Sack has been here over twenty years, and there were a series of nannies, most of whose names I can't even remember.'

I had mixed emotions. On the one hand, I wanted to gain a better understanding of what had shaped Erica Marshall, why she was so bitter toward her father. On the other hand, intensely personal family matters made me uncomfortable. And, of course, the murder of Matilda Swift was certainly center stage this night.

Erica's eyes were flashing. She was wide awake now. She stood and went to the coffeemaker. The red light was on, indicating the brewing was completed.

'I didn't mean to upset you,' I said, joining her at the counter and helping to arrange cups on two trays.

'Everyone always worries about my father. "Poor Paul, having to raise a child by himself." "Poor Paul, losing his best friend and partner." "Poor Paul." "Poor Paul."' Her voice had taken on a singsong sound. 'Poor Paul, my foot,' she said, stamping on the tile floor. 'He's hard as nails. He only pretends to miss Tony. Nothing gets to him.'

Still fuming, she filled two carafes and wrenched open the refrigerator door, pulling out a container of milk and setting it down hard on one of the trays, next to a sugar bowl.

'We'll save the niceties for another time, shall we,' she said sharply, lifting a tray and turning from me.

\*         \*         \*

Wendell had completed his task of getting basic information from everyone when I reached the living room and placed my tray down next to Erica's on the French writing table. Everyone perked up at the promise of caffeine and poured themselves cups of coffee. I did, too, but only a half cup—I still held out hope for a few hours' sleep later on—and resumed my seat by the fireplace, near Seth Hazlitt. Erica sat in a Chippendale chair far removed from her two angry pursuers. Her legs were crossed at the ankle, and one foot bounced up and down at a fast tempo.

'Mrs. Fletcher?'

'Yes, Wendell?'

'I know who you are and all,' he said, smiling sheepishly. 'I figure I don't need to ask you questions.'

'Oh, I think you'd better get a complete record for Sheriff Metzger, Wendell. Ask me whatever you've been asking the others.'

'I suppose you're right, ma'am.' He pulled a

pencil from his uniform jacket pocket and opened a spiral-bound pad.

'What would you like to know?' I asked, placing my cup and saucer down and looking into his earnest face.

As I spelled my complete name for him, he carefully printed it with the kind of neat penmanship his grade school teachers would have been proud to see. He wrote my name, address and telephone number, each on a separate line in his narrow notebook, then looked up at me. 'You're not planning to go out of town any time soon, are you, Mrs. Fletcher?'

'No, Wendell. I'll be in Cabot Cove through Thanksgiving. I may take a day or two in New York in December to see my agent and do some holiday shopping, but if the investigation is still going on, and you and the sheriff say so, I can put off the trip.'

A worried look crossed Wendell's brow. 'I sure hope we've solved the murder before then.'

'We all hope that,' I agreed.

Mort returned a few minutes later. The cool draft that came through the French doors with him freshened the air, and the sounds of rustling clothes and clearing throats indicated that everyone was ready for what would come next.

'Sheriff,' Robert Wandowski said from his corner of the room, 'can you question me first?

103

My wife must be frantic by now.'

'Why don't you give her a call?' Harold suggested. 'I'm sure Mr. Marshall won't mind.'

Paul looked at his employee as if surprised to see him still here. 'No, no, of course not. Go ahead, Bob.'

Wandowski shook his head. 'Can't do that. I'd wake my daughter. She's a light sleeper. Then I'd have two hysterical females to deal with when I get home. C'mon, Sheriff. You've got to start with someone. I barely know most of these people, and I sure didn't know that lady, either, hardly at all. Only time I ever saw her you were there, and—'

Joan interrupted. 'Look here, Sheriff, he's not the only one who wants to go home.'

'I think we should go in alphabetical order,' Jack Decker said, grinning.

'I'll decide who goes first,' Mort said. 'Mr. Marshall, is there another room I can use for interviews, some place private?'

'There's the library,' Paul said. 'I'll show you where it is.'

Mort and Harold followed Marshall out into the hall, and Wendell moved to stand by the exit. Silence descended once again as everyone collapsed back into their seats.

I watched as Lucas Tremaine surveyed the guests from his vantage point in the center of the room. Wisps of his long hair had escaped from its leather thong, and a five o'clock shadow—it was now well after midnight—

considerably darkened his cheeks and jaw. Even in the headless moose costume, he was a commanding presence. He could have been handsome; his features were fine, almost pretty, but there was a hardness to his face that contradicted them. The expression in his gray eyes was derisive and calculating. I wondered what he was thinking.

Paul Marshall returned, paused at the doorway, then went to his seat, carrying a book.

'Might as well read something while I'm waiting,' he said.

'Are there more where that came from?' Joan asked.

'You wouldn't have any magazines back there, would you?' Marilou Decker said.

Paul's response was to take out a pair of half glasses, open the small volume, and, ignoring everyone, begin to read.

Harold reappeared and came to me. 'The sheriff would like to see you, Mrs. Fletcher.'

'Damn, he didn't listen to a thing I said.' Bob Wandowski spat, smacking his right fist into his left palm, then resuming his pacing in the corner.

I followed Harold to the front hall and down a wide corridor, the clicking of our heels on the rose-colored marble floor echoing off the vaulted ceiling. We stopped before a pair of carved walnut doors with large brass knobs. Harold pushed one open and stepped aside, allowing me to enter. He followed and closed the door behind us.

Paul Marshall's library was lovely. I'd been in it before for one civic meeting or another, but it never failed to warm me. Two dozen cherrywood bookcases holding thousands of books dominated three walls. I knew from previous visits that one shelf held several well-thumbed mysteries by J. B. Fletcher, as well as books of the same genre by Agatha Christie and P. D. James. Heady company.

Mort had taken the high-backed chair behind Paul Marshall's desk. He looked tired but determined, and a little silly in his party costume. I realized I must look silly, too. 'The Legend' was still walking but definitely bedraggled, and I felt the sudden need to remove the gray fright wig and give my face a good scrubbing. Mort must have read my mind. 'There's a lavatory through there, Mrs. F., if you want to wash up,' he said, indicating a door in the corner.

I made my escape, returning a few minutes later with my own coiffure, albeit a bit flattened, and my natural complexion.

'That's better,' I said, taking a seat in a leather armchair and dropping the wig in my lap. I fished my reading glasses out of my pocket and looped the cord attached to the earpieces around my neck.

Mort got down to business. 'Mrs. F., did you know the deceased?'

'We'd never been introduced, Mort, but I'd seen her several times around town.'

'When was the last time you saw her?'

'I saw her across the school foyer right after the Halloween pageant and before that, I believe was when you went to investigate the report of the missing Wandowski child and I tagged along. As you know, we hardly spoke with her at the time.'

'She was kind of a contradiction, wasn't she?' Mort mused, making a note to himself. 'She had those cold eyes, but she baked cookies with the little girl.'

'Some people find it easier to communicate with children than they do with other adults. Perhaps she was lonely, and the child offered her a bit of companionship.'

'Maybe. See anything out of the ordinary tonight?'

'Other than a hundred people in costumes and masks?'

Mort looked down at his fringed shirt and shook his head. 'Any ideas where we should start with that group out there?'

'We?'

'I hate to keep you up, but I'd be obliged if you'd stay in here and listen to what they have to say. Wouldn't be the first time you picked up on something I missed. I mean, that hasn't happened often, but I just figured—'

'Of course, Mort. You know I'll do anything to help.'

'Let's do some of this in batches before we have a revolt on our hands,' he said. 'Harold, bring in the Lerners. And give these car keys to my wife.' To me: 'If Maureen doesn't get some sleep tonight, I'll feel the sharp side of her tongue tomorrow. She's got a meeting of the School Lunch Committee first thing in the morning.'

'Sure you want to interview couples together?' I asked. 'I thought you always preferred one-on-one interviews.'

'I do, Mrs. F., under most circumstances. But considering the time of night, and the fact that the couples we know wouldn't be murdering anybody, I'd like to get it over with as fast as possible. Just want to know what they might have seen.'

I removed my shawl, folded it over the wig, got up and went to a cushioned window seat. As an unofficial observer, I wanted to be as unobtrusive as possible. Mort was right. It was unlikely that one of our group was a murderer. Except for the Lerners, who were recent arrivals, we'd known one another for years. But perhaps someone did see something that would provide a clue to the perpetrator. Of course, I didn't know Wandowski to speak to, and certainly not Tremaine. It would be interesting to hear what they had to say.

Harold escorted Joan and Ed Lerner into the room, followed by Mort's wife, Maureen. All that was left of her elaborate makeup were dark arcs under her eyes where the mascara had smudged. 'Sure you want me to leave?' she asked.

'Yup, you go on home, honey. I can ask you all the questions I need to over breakfast.' He grinned. She came behind the desk, kissed him on the cheek and left.

Mort said to Harold, 'Go see how the state cops are doing down at the crime scene. And check to make sure Jerry has enough guys to cover the shifts guarding the taped area.'

'Sure thing, Sheriff.'

Mort repeated to the Lerners the few questions he'd asked me. Ed Lerner tried, and failed, to stifle a series of yawns. He gave Mort a wan smile and said, 'I'm not much of a witness, Sheriff. I can't think of anything that would be helpful. We never even met the lady who was killed. What about you, Joan?'

'Well, let me think,' his wife said. 'You know, we're new here, so we don't know everyone. And with all the costumes, especially the moose ones . . .' Her eyes narrowed as she concentrated on the evening's events. Being a witness in a murder investigation had given her a second wind. I raised my glasses and glanced at my watch. It was two-thirty.

'I do recall seeing one of the moose walking away from the party. I remember wondering why he was leaving so early,' she said.

'And where did you see this moose?' Mort asked.

109

'Well, he was walking toward the cemetery. I didn't know about the cemetery then, but I do now, since we ran through it before finding the body. I think that must be why I counted them—the moose, you know—when we were down at the cottage. There were so many of them around. I kept seeing them everywhere I looked.'

'Do you have any idea what time that was? The moose in the cemetery.' Mort tapped his pencil on his pad.

'I'd say sometime right after dinner was served. Isn't that right, Ed?'

Her husband shrugged. 'I don't remember that,' he said, yawning.

'That must have been when you were talking about camera lenses with the photographer,' she said.

'That I remember. Nice guy. I invited him to our party next month,' Ed Lerner said.

'I'm glad you told me,' Joan said. 'I want to start working on the guest list tomorrow.'

'I also invited the Deckers and the Walters. Okay with you?'

Mort cleared his throat.

'Sorry, Sheriff,' Ed said, grinning. 'I didn't mean to get us off the topic, but you see, we're having a Veteran's Day party next month.'

'And we certainly hope you and Maureen can make it,' Joan added.

Mort looked confused. 'Sure, thanks.'

'Joan, are you sure you didn't see a *pair* of

moose?' I asked from my perch, pulling them back to the matter at hand. I remembered the moose couple in the moonlight. 'And could it have been before dinner?'

Joan stared at me, but her eyes were focused inward as she tried to recall the sequence of events. 'Nooo,' she said, drawing the word out softly. 'I'm sure it was later, Jessica. We'd gotten our plates from the buffet, then stopped to admire Miss Havisham's table. Wasn't that a wonderful literary reference, Ed?'

She sensed Mort's growing impatience. 'Sorry,' she said, 'I seem to be losing my place.'

'It's late, Mrs. Lerner,' Mort said. 'Go on.'

'Well, we couldn't find an empty place at any of the tables inside, so we went out onto the patio. It was very warm inside anyway with the crush of the crowd. The photographer was out there and a few others, and the only seats available were along the stone wall that overlooks the grounds. I remember seeing a moose walking, striding really, across the lawn. Then I sat down, so my back was to him, and I didn't see anything else.'

'You said "him,"' Mort pointed out. 'Are you sure it was a man?'

'Actually, with those huge heads on, it was impossible to tell. And we were too far away to gauge height, so I don't really know if it was a man. I suppose it could have been a woman.'

Harold knocked and pushed open the door. Behind him in the hall was a state patrolman.

Mort thanked the Lerners for their cooperation and handed them a card with his office phone number. 'Please give me a call if you think of anything else. Sometimes folks remember things when they're more relaxed and have a chance to sleep on it. And I'd appreciate your not discussing this investigation with anyone else.'

The Lerners agreed and left the room.

'Okay, Harold, bring in the Deckers and the Walters,' Mort said.

'What about Tremaine?' I asked. 'He's the only uninvited guest.'

'I'm saving Mr. Tremaine for last.'

Harold disappeared into the hall. A moment later, the door to the library slammed back against the wall and Robert Wandowski stalked into the room, his face a mask of fury. Harold, a hand on his right shoulder, was right behind him. 'Couldn't help this, Sheriff,' the deputy said. 'He pushed right past me.'

The hulking Wandowski came directly to the desk, then put large hands on it and leaned over Mort. 'I gotta get home. You know how late it is? You ignored me.'

Mort asked Harold, 'You okay?'

'Yeah,' Harold said, rubbing his shoulder.

Mort stood and faced Wandowski. 'You sit down, sir, and don't get up till I tell you to or I'll have you taken in for impeding an investigation and assaulting a peace officer.' He turned to Harold: 'You keep an eye on him. If he moves, cuff him.'

Wandowski's jaw dropped, and his bravado seemed to ooze out of him. 'Look, I'm sitting down,' he said. 'I won't move, Sheriff, I promise. I'm sorry. I just get a little hot now and then.'

'I'm not the one you should be apologizing to,' Mort said.

'Sorry, Hal.'

'What was that?' Mort said.

'I said, "Sorry, Hal."'

'You two know each other?' Mort asked his deputy.

'We're in the same bowling league,' Harold said. He looked at Wandowski: 'Just cooperate with the sheriff, Bob, and don't make any more trouble.'

Mort moved to the front of the desk, then leaned back on the polished walnut and cherry inlaid top and glared down at Wandowski, who squirmed in his chair. Mort let the silence build, keeping his gaze on Wandowski, who glanced over his shoulder at Harold, looked down at the carpet, then up again, his eyes unable to meet Mort's. The tension grew, and I watched Wandowski's face turn red, pale, then red again. Finally, he blew, as Mort knew he would.

'I didn't do it!' he exclaimed. 'I was here all night. I never left the party.'

'You were angry with her.'

'I swear I didn't do it.'

113

'You were getting even.'

'No, no, you're wrong.'

'You threatened her right in front of me.'

'I know, but I swear I never saw her again.'

'You just said yourself you can't control your temper. You saw her and remembered your daughter coming out of her cottage. You felt the rage all over again. And you killed her.'

'No! You can't trick me into saying anything. I'm not the killer.'

'You just wanted to protect your home, right?' Harold said kindly. 'You just wanted to keep your family safe.'

Wandowski looked up, relieved at the show of support from the deputy. 'Yes,' he sighed. 'Of course I want to keep my family safe.'

'So you killed Ms. Swift because she represented a threat to their safety.' Mort's voice was low and measured.

'No, no, I didn't say that.'

'You thought she'd kidnapped your, daughter, and you wanted to get even.' Mort slapped the desktop, punctuating his lines. 'You wanted to kill her. You didn't want her anywhere near your daughter. She was a stranger, different—everyone said so. She was evil, luring your daughter into her cottage when you weren't there. What was she doing to your girl? She was—'

Wandowski leapt to his feet. 'She never should have taken Julie!' he roared. 'She got what she deserved.'

Mort stopped and eyed Wandowski. I held my breath.

Wandowski looked around frantically. 'No, no, I know it sounds like I was mad at her, and I was, I was, but I didn't kill her. I swear.' He collapsed back into his seat and wrapped his arms about himself.

I let out the breath I'd been holding. Mort shrugged and looked at Harold. The deputy put a hand on Wandowski's shoulder. 'All right, Bob, calm down now.'

Mort turned his back on them and went to the door. 'You can go home, Wandowski, but I'm not through talking to you. You're not to leave Cabot Cove. Understand?'

Wandowski nodded.

'Mr. Wandowski,' I said from my observation post at the window, 'may I ask you a question?'

Wandowski appeared surprised. He must have forgotten I was there. 'Yes, ma'am,' he said.

'Why didn't your wife come to the party with you tonight?'

'Uh, she wanted to, but we didn't have a baby-sitter for my daughter. I work for Mr. Marshall, so I had to come, even if she couldn't.'

'Go on, go home,' Mort said. Wandowski slowly stood and shuffled from the room in stark contrast to the way he'd entered.

The Deckers were next to be interviewed.

'You folks are in the business of noticing things,' Mort said, 'being writers and publishers and all. What'd you see tonight?'

Jack Decker, a tall, handsome man with a deep voice, laughed gently. 'I'm afraid we didn't have our journalist ears and eyes operating tonight, Mort. We were strictly here to enjoy ourselves.'

Marilou added, 'Jack is right, but I can't imagine that poor woman's murder has anything to do with the party. It had to have been someone passing through, some nut.'

'Or someone who knew her but wasn't at the party,' her husband said.

'You may be right,' said Mort, 'but I can't go on assumptions like that. What do you know about Ms. Swift?'

The Deckers looked at each other before Marilou said, 'All I know is that there's been a lot of talk about her since she moved here. People considered her strange.'

'Strange how?' Mort asked.

'Different, I suppose is the way to describe it,' Marilou replied. 'Some people can be cruel when a newcomer arrives who doesn't look like the rest of us.'

How true, I thought.

Jack said, 'I've been told that Ms. Swift had been asking around about Tony Scott's death in the fire.'

I sat up a little straighter. So did Mort.

'Why was she doing that?' Mort asked.

Jack shrugged. 'Idle curiosity, I suppose.'

'Happened a year ago,' said Mort. 'Can't imagine why a stranger to town would be wondering about that.'

I interjected, 'Who did she ask about it, Jack?'

'Dick Mann for one.' Dick is Cabot Cove's fire chief.

Mort made a note. 'Anyone else?' he asked.

The Deckers shook their heads.

'Well, folks, thanks for sharing what you know,' Mort said. 'Might as well go home and get to bed.'

I smiled as the Deckers stood and left the library. Since coming to Cabot Cove after successful careers in magazine publishing in New York, they'd become one of the town's most popular couples, erudite and attractive, involved and concerned.

Harold escorted Pete and Roberta Walters into the room. They owned a small radio station that provided soothing music and lots of local news.

'How about a statement for the record, Mort?' Pete asked. 'I'm heading for the station once we leave here.'

Mort closed his eyes and pinched the bridge of his nose. 'The only statement I can give is that there's been a murder, and that our office is investigating. I'd appreciate it, Pete, if you held off on reporting any of this for twenty-four hours, till after I finish the interviews.'

'Mort, you know how unrealistic that is. The word will be all over town by sunup, and the TV and newspapers will be on the case not long after that. Sorry, Mort, but I can't do it.'

'Well then, no speculating, huh? Just stick to the facts. And if anyone calls with information about the case, give 'em this number.' He handed Pete a card.

'Of course.'

'I know you're used to asking the questions, Pete,' Mort said, 'but when there's a murder, I do the asking.'

'Shoot,' Pete said.

'Roberta, you and Pete were here all evening. See anything unusual, anything might shed some light on what happened down at the Rose Cottage?'

'Can't say that I did,' she responded.

'You, Pete?'

'No. The only thing I saw were people having a good time. What's your read on it, Mort? I assume that nut out there, Tremaine, is at the top of your suspect list.'

'I don't have such a list yet. You have any contact with the victim since she moved here?'

They both denied having ever met Matilda. But then Pete said, 'I heard she was down at the newspaper, looking through clips in the morgue.'

'That so?' Mort said. 'Know what she was looking for?'

118

'Horace told me she was diggin' into articles on Tony Scott's death.'

Mort glanced at me before asking, 'How come Horace wasn't at the party?' Horace Teller is publisher of the *Cabot Cove News*, our weekly newspaper.

'Out of town,' Roberta answered. 'Visiting his son in New York.'

'I see,' Mort said. 'Well, unless you've got anything else to say, you're free to go.'

'Sure I can't get a statement from you, Mort?'

'Yup, I'm sure. Safe home.'

Harold escorted the Walters out of the library, and Mort placed his elbows on the desk and rested his head in his palms.

'Don't you think it's time to call it a night?' I suggested, getting up to stretch my legs. My right foot had fallen asleep.

'Can't leave just yet, Mrs. F. The others I can get to later, but Mr. Tremaine has some questions to answer, plenty of 'em.'

'Of course,' I said. 'Shall I go tell everyone they're free to leave, and have Harold or Wendell bring Mr. Tremaine in?'

'Thanks, Mrs. F., I appreciate the help. By the way, I'm intending to inspect the cottage tomorrow.' He massaged his neck and rolled his head. 'I'll be back out here around ten. You're welcome, as usual, to join me.'

'I'll take you up on that, Mort. I'm interested in seeing Ms. Swift's home. You

119

learn a lot about people from the way they live.'

The occupants of the Marshall living room were barely awake when I entered. Wendell was close to falling asleep on his feet, arms crossed, head leaning against the wall. Paul Marshall stared into space, his book resting on his chest, half glasses perched on his nose. His daughter had drawn her chair up to the French writing table; a pillow from the sofa cushioned her dark head on the table's sleek surface. Her two swain, if that's what they were, sat slumped on sofas on opposite sides of the room, fighting to keep their eyes open. And Seth snored, not so gently, in his wing chair. The scene was peaceful, if a bit noisy, but something was not right. The room was chilly, and I noticed the patio doors were ajar. And then I realized immediately what was amiss. The chair in which Lucas Tremaine had been sitting was empty.

He was gone.

## CHAPTER EIGHT

The sun came up far too early the next day, even for this usually early-to-bed, early-to-rise lady. I'd been early to bed, all right, but it had been early in the morning, not early in the evening. I was contemplating getting out of bed when the ringing of the telephone jangled my nerves and forced me upright.

'Mrs. F.?'

'Good morning, Mort. At least I think it's a good morning.'

'I take it you and the doc got home all right.'

'Yes, we did, and I was happy to be here. Did you find Mr. Tremaine?'

'Ayuh. Got to be one of the strangest characters I've ever met. He sneaks away from the scene of the murder but doesn't go very far. Wendell and Jerry hightail it over to that place he calls his spiritual headquarters and there he is, sitting on a chair out front waiting for them. Gives them a big greeting and says he figures they're there to get him, walks over to the squad car, gets in and says, "Let's go."'

'Where is he now?'

'In jail. I'm holding him as a material witness. I can only hold him for so long. Would have to charge him with Ms. Swift's murder or some other crime to keep him any longer. That's the law.'

'Did you question him?'

'We had a few words last night when they brought him in. He says he crashed the party because he likes good parties. He's a smug son-of-a-gun. I asked him why he left, and he said he got bored. Always got a big smile. Gives me the creeps.'

'Have you spoken with anyone else this morning?'

'Got a call from Paul Marshall. He's coming in to talk to me this afternoon.'

'That's good. What about the young people—Erica, Jeremy and Warren?'

'Not sure if they'll be coming with Marshall or not. Marshall said he has to go out of town on business. Wants to "get this over with" were his words.'

'How long does he plan to be gone?'

'Said two or three days. Intends leaving after we have our talk. What do you think?'

'I wouldn't worry about him, Mort. He has his daughter and business here.'

'That's the way I figure it.'

'Did he mention if he was taking Warren Wilson with him?'

'Didn't say. Well, just wanted to let you know I'm heading for the Rose Cottage. Still planning on joining me?'

'I'll be there,' I said, pushing my toes into my slippers and lifting my robe from the foot of the bed, 'but it'll take me a half hour or so to put myself together.'

'No rush,' he said. 'You come on along whenever you can. I'll be there a while. I'll bring a Thermos of coffee, now that you taught me how to make it.'

'Sounds fine. Would you like me to stop off for doughnuts on my way?'

'Sure thing. Doughnuts are one of the basic food groups in law enforcement.'

I laughed and rang off. Tying the belt of my

122

robe, I started for the kitchen when something stopped me. I looked back at the phone. What was it? I replayed our conversation in my mind, but there was nothing out of the ordinary there. Maybe after I showered my mind would be a little clearer, I decided.

*     *     *

Sassi's Bakery was buzzing with news of the murder when I arrived on my bike. Brenda Brody, who worked for the Cabot Cove magazine, was there buying a coffee cake.

'I know you don't believe in such things, Jessica,' she said with a sniff, 'but Lucas Tremaine predicted that The Legend would rise up and terrible plagues would descend on Cabot Cove, and just look what's happened. It's happening just the way he said it would.'

'Brenda, tragic as it is, one murder could hardly be considered a plague. And no spirit wielded the weapon that killed Matilda Swift.'

'And what's making the dogs howl every night? Dogs are sensitive to ghosts, you know.'

'Never having encountered a ghost and a dog at the same time, I'm afraid my experience is limited.'

'You can scoff, but Mr. Tremaine has been very helpful to me. I believe he has a direct line into the spirit world, and I'm not the only one who thinks so.'

Direct line! That was what I was trying to

123

remember this morning. 'I'm sorry to break off this conversation, Brenda, but I've got to run. Nice seeing you.'

Mort was already at the Rose Cottage when I arrived carrying a bag of doughnuts. He was holding a clipboard and making notes.

'The state guys finished dusting the place, and we've got lots of Polaroids and a video, so we don't have to worry about disturbing the scene,' he said as I followed him down the hall into the combination kitchen-dining room.

'You know what occurred to me this morning after I spoke with you?' I said, arranging the doughnuts on a plate.

'What's that?' Mort picked up a powdered doughnut, one of his favorites I knew.

'It was the telephone line.'

'Ayuh, what about it?' He took a bite.

'It was clear,' I said. 'There was no static. That was the first phone call in weeks in which I didn't have to fight to have my voice heard over the noise on the line.'

Mort chewed thoughtfully and swallowed. 'That's right. Funny, it happening right after Ms. Swift got killed.'

'I can't imagine there's a connection,' I said. 'I'm sure the telephone company has fixed the problem. But it did cross my mind.' I debated a doughnut and decided to forgo the extra calories. 'Where do we start?' I asked.

'I'm going to check out the kitchen area,' Mort said, eying the doughnut plate. 'Why don't you look around and see if there's a desk where she kept her papers.'

A decorator's touch was evident in the main room. It was naturally cozy, given its small size, but also exhibited a certain sophistication. Large pink flowers on a chintz fabric covered the loveseat and matching armchair positioned in front of the brick-and-stone fireplace. The furniture was placed on a rose-patterned rug that snuggled up to the flagstone hearth and polished brass fender. Red-and-pink striped curtains were pulled back with brass rosettes, and embroidered red and pink roses were sprinkled across the upholstered valance. The effect could have been cloying, but the professional hired by Paul Marshall knew just when to pull back. The coffee table and side tables were burnished walnut, and their dark wood contrasted boldly with the flowery theme, saving the room from being too sweet. I reminded myself I was not here to admire the decor, and studied the remainder of the room, looking for clues to Matilda Swift's personality and, more important, to why someone would want her dead.

While Mort took inventory in the kitchen, I sat down on the loveseat. There was no desk in the room, but on the coffee table in front of me was a large green lacquered box. I lifted the lid and was surprised to find several stacks of envelopes arranged by date and secured with rubber bands. Matilda Swift didn't get much mail, I thought, if she was able to keep it in a decorative box. I flipped through the envelopes and contemplated opening some. I suffered a natural reluctance to read someone else's mail. I certainly wouldn't want strangers going through my papers and personal items. But, I reminded myself, this is an unusual circumstance. A killer was at large. Were Matilda Swift able to speak for herself, I was sure she'd tell us she wanted her killer found and brought to justice.

I examined the mail. The pieces were mostly bank statements and invoices that she'd marked 'paid' in a bold hand. They included her rent and utility bills, telephone, life insurance and cable television. In the 'to be paid' pile, there was a bill from Charles Department Store for gardening supplies, and another from a local market for groceries, but nothing from credit card companies. The mail was evidence of a modest life, and I wondered if she'd always lived that way. I pulled out one envelope and put it in my pocket. Drawing papers from one of the statements, I scanned the column of figures. The accompanying cashed checks corresponded to the bills I'd already seen. I replaced the statement in the pile and pulled out the next one. I continued reading until Mort emerged from the kitchen.

'Find anything?' he asked, leaning over the back of the loveseat to see what was in my hand.

126

'I may have,' I replied, lifting up a statement I'd put aside. 'See this bank charge?'

'Ayuh.'

'It's for a safe-deposit box. Did you find any keys in the kitchen?'

'Didn't see any. You think they'd be there?'

'There's no table in the hall, so my guess is she'd keep her keys in the kitchen.'

We trooped into the kitchen and went to a four-drawer cabinet.

'Already checked these,' he said. 'Guess it won't hurt to look again.'

The top drawer held flatware and a few small utensils. The one beneath it was filled with basic kitchen paraphernalia—knives, spatulas, wooden spoons and the like. Drawers three and four were occupied respectively by potholders and dish towels, boxes of plastic garbage and storage bags, aluminum foil, plastic wrap and wax paper. We examined the contents of each drawer carefully—no keys.

'Everyone I know has a junk drawer in the kitchen,' I said, 'or some other box or container for all the little things you want to keep but don't know where to put.'

'Maureen keeps coupons and thumbtacks and extra keys, stuff like that, in a big cookie jar.'

We both eyed a white china canister on the counter. Mort flipped the latch that held it closed and peered inside. Smiling, he reached into it and withdrew a large chocolate chip

127

cookie. 'Want one?' he asked. 'Maureen's got me on a diet.'

'I'll pass,' I said, methodically opening and closing the kitchen cabinets, not sure what I was looking for. In a tall, narrow pantry were several more canisters matching the cookie jar. I picked one up, shook it, and looked inside. Tea bags. The next one rattled when I pulled it off the shelf. I grabbed a dish towel from the third drawer, laid it on the countertop and tipped the canister contents onto it.

'Why'd you need a dish towel?' Mort asked, standing next to me at the counter.

'So nothing will roll away,' I responded, looking over my cache. There were a few keys, empty key rings, magnets advertising local shopkeepers, a child's yo-yo, an old screwdriver, six pennies, some folded brown paper and a leaky pen. Trying unsuccessfully to avoid getting ink on my fingers, I picked out three keys from the collection. Two were of the old-fashioned skeleton key variety; the third looked like it might fit the front door lock. No safe-deposit box key. I picked up the brown paper and carefully unfolded it. It was half of a tiny envelope. The letters 'ANK' were stamped in black ink.

'I think we've found where the key may have been, but it's not here now,' I said, handing the torn envelope to him and refilling the canister.

Mort stared at the envelope. 'She had a couple of keys in her pocket the night she was

128

killed. I bagged them and put them in the evidence file.'

'If one of them is a safe-deposit box key, will you have trouble convincing the bank to open the box for you?'

'Don't know for sure. I'll have to get a judge to agree.'

'That could take some time,' I said.

'No. Judge Kaplan'll issue the order pretty quick, it being a murder investigation.'

'If it's the key,' I reminded him.

'I'll give Marie a call at the station and have her look in the evidence closet.'

Marie Poutre was one of Mort's deputies, and pretty much ran headquarters for him. Not only was she highly organized, she was the best-read cop I'd ever met, including every text book available on police procedure and investigations. She consumed dozens of murder mysteries every month, including mine, and I'd developed such respect for her knowledge and insight that I'd established a routine of giving her a copy of my manuscripts for her evaluation of how I'd handled police procedural matters.

While Mort made his call, I pulled a small garbage pail from beneath the sink and peered into it. It was virtually empty, just a few pieces of wadded-up paper towel, no scraps of food. I pushed the paper towel aside, saw something else, reached in and extracted a cigar stub that had been extinguished with water, probably held beneath a faucet. Cuban? Impossible for a nonsmoker to tell without the cigar band.

'Mort,' I called, straining to hear if he was off the phone, 'come look at this.'

'Yup. Coming,' he said, stepping into the room.

'Do you think Matilda smoked cigars?'

He laughed. 'Not likely.'

'I found this in the trash.'

As he placed the stub in a small plastic evidence bag, I washed my hands and went into Matilda's bedroom. The same air of country elegance that made the living room so inviting was also evident there. Pastel stripes and solids with the occasional plaid created a restful feeling. A cherry four-poster dominated the room, with matching cabinets flanking the bed, serving as both nightstands and dressers. In one corner a chaise with an afghan thrown across the back was positioned next to a window. In the other corner was a standing oval mirror tilted slightly on its axis.

A residue of white fingerprint powder clung to the front of the cabinet drawers, contrasting with the silky deep red wood. I was still drying my hands and used the dish towel to open the drawers. I leaned against the side of the bed and studied the jumble that had been Matilda's clothing. Mort joined me.

'When the officers dusted for fingerprints, did they conduct a search of the premises as well?' I asked him.

'Nope. That's what we're here for.'

'Look at these drawers,' I said. 'We just came from an immaculate kitchen and tidy living room. Doesn't it strike you as odd that someone who would be so neat in one part of her house would treat her clothing like this?' Every drawer was partially open. 'Would your men have left them open?'

'Absolutely not,' he said. 'Aside from the state cops dusting for prints, this cottage was off-limits until I got here this morning. Nothing was searched last night, including those drawers or the closet. I was just getting set to take a look at them.'

'Well, Mort, if I were a gambler, I'd wager that Matilda Swift's drawers have been searched, either between the time of the murder and now, or before she died—maybe just before she died.'

I eyed her closet door. 'Let's take a look in there,' I said, moving across the room and using the dish towel to turn the knob. The clothes hanging on the rod had been roughly pushed to one side, and several hangers had tumbled to the floor along with the skirts and jackets they held, some covered by plastic film from a dry cleaning establishment.

'Either someone has been here before us,' I speculated, 'or Matilda caught someone searching this room.'

'The killer?'

'Possibly. She might have run outside for

help.'

I shivered, remembering how much I looked like Matilda Swift in my Legend costume. Was she fighting for her life while I, her double, was eating and drinking at a party? I preferred not to think about it.

'Oh, did you reach your dispatcher?'

'I did. She checked the evidence envelopes, says there's a small key looks to her like it would fit a bank safe-deposit box.'

'That's good news,' I said. 'When are you going to take it to the bank?'

'This afternoon, after I talk to Paul Marshall. I suppose you'd like to come along.'

'As a matter fact, I would. Okay with you?'

'Always is. I already checked the medicine cabinet in the bathroom and the closet in the front hall, so looks like we've given this place a pretty good going-over.'

'I want to take a look around outside,' I said.

'You go ahead, Mrs. F. I'll go through those drawers again. You've got me thinking.'

'Oh, Mort, I almost forgot,' I said, pulling out the envelope I'd tucked in my pocket earlier. I handed it to him. 'This is a bill from her life insurance company. You probably should find out who her beneficiary is.'

'Good idea, Mrs. F.'

*     *     *

I stood in front of the Rose Cottage and looked up at the sky. It had a winter look to it, slate gray and cold, unforgiving. I wished I'd dressed more warmly, added another layer. My arms wrapped about myself, I scanned the five-foot-high brick wall against which award-winning roses burst forth in spring and summer. The mulch Artie Sack had laid down was perfectly edged and mounded, which didn't surprise me. Each time he did work at my house, I was always impressed with how meticulous he was. Nothing was ever out of place, every flower bed edged with a sharp, precise line, my few climbing rose bushes tied neatly to their trellises, the twist ties all secured with the same number of turns and tucked out of sight.

The spray paint outline of Matilda Swift's body was still vivid on the ground, and I gave it a wide berth as I walked along the wall and took a look behind the cottage. There was nothing back there except her long black car parked beneath the graceful boughs of a tall elm tree. I peered inside the car and saw it was locked. I also observed that there wasn't anything in the vehicle that shouldn't be there, no empty drinking cup or loose change or stray piece of clothing. Neat, like the cottage, except for the drawers and closet in her bedroom.

I came back around to the front of the cottage and looked across the expanse of lawn to a small barn three hundred feet or so from

133

where I stood. I headed for it, walking slowly, looking left and right in search of . . . in search of nothing specific. To my right and up a rolling hill were the small cemetery and Paul Marshall's baronial mansion standing staunch and impenetrable in the gray morning light, the scene of such gaiety the previous night, now a somber symbol of murder that had occurred within shouting distance of the party-goers.

As I came closer to the barn, I saw that Artie Sack was in front of it. He was busy with a task, although I couldn't determine what it was from my vantage point. When I was only a few yards from him, he realized I was there and looked up from the scythe he was sharpening with a whetstone. He jumped and looked around as though he wanted to bolt.

'Hello, Artie,' I said pleasantly.

'Hello Mrs. Fletcher, Hello Mrs. Fletcher.' He averted his eyes and went back to sharpening the long, curved scythe.

'Terrible what happened to Matilda Swift last night. Did you know her well?'

'I work for Mr. Paul. Mr. Paul is good to me, good,' he mumbled.

'I'm sure Paul Marshall appreciates what a fine gardener you are. Did Matilda Swift also appreciate your rose garden?'

Artie shuffled his feet, still holding the huge scythe upright. 'She was a nice lady, nice lady. She liked to garden, too.' He looked across the lawn toward the roses, then ducked his head and began drawing the stone across the blade again.

'Sheriff Metzger and I have been looking around the Rose Cottage,' I said. 'Have you found anything unusual around here this morning?'

'Unusual? No ma'am, no ma'am.'

I took a few steps toward the door of the barn, but Artie dropped the scythe and grinding stone to the ground and stepped in front of me.

I looked at him quizzically.

'Nothing in there, Mrs. Fletcher. You'll get yourself all dirty, all dirty.'

'I am used to getting dirty, Artie. A little dirt on the hands is honest. What do you keep in here?'

'Just tools, Mrs. Fletcher.'

'Well, thanks for worrying about me, but I'll be fine.' When he realized I intended to enter the barn, he lowered his head and trudgcd back to his scythe.

Strange, I thought. He really didn't want me to go in. I opened the door and allowed my eyes to adjust to the darkness. Slim rays of light came through gaps in the barn's siding, painting jagged patterns over the walls and dirt floor.

I stepped inside. To the rear of the barn was a tractor, two commercial-sized power mowers and a few carts used to move gardening supplies around the estate. An old milk crate on the floor just to my right held a pile of rags; they were obviously dirty but folded neatly all the same. Behind the crate, stacked to the ceiling against the wall, was firewood, as neatly arranged as the tools hanging on the opposite wall. I went to the tools and looked closely at a few of them. There were shovels of various shapes and sizes, rakes, edging tools, hedge clippers, gardening trowels and other implements you'd expect to find. Pairs of garden gloves, arranged by size, nestled in a basket hanging from a hook.

I couldn't help but shake my head and smile at the meticulous care Artie took with everything. The tools were wiped clean and oiled, not a shred of grass or dirt on any of them. I was about to turn and leave when one of the shovels, a long-handled model with a pointed blade, caught my eye. It was even cleaner than the others, its blade gleaming as though it had just been polished. Keeping tools clean was one thing, but polishing a shovel? That seemed to carry things a little too far, even for someone as orderly as Artie Sack.

I pulled a pair of gloves from the basket, put them on, and took the shovel from the wall. The business end was without blemish. But when I looked more closely at the juncture where the wooden handle joined the metal blade, there was a trace of something there. It's probably rust, I told myself. I'm no forensic scientist, but still, I wondered, could that rust be blood?

Now where did I see those rags? I replaced the shovel on the wall and went to where the milk crate was placed near the open door. Still wearing the gloves, I reached down and picked up what had once been a white cloth and sniffed it—distinctly oil and gasoline. I perused others until I reached a rag whose rust-colored stains had not originated with oil or gas. Again, blood came to mind.

I replaced the gloves where I'd found them and left the barn. Artie was nowhere about, but the sharpened scythe was leaning against the side of the barn. Mort was just finishing up at the Rose Cottage when I walked in. 'Mort,' I said, 'I'd like you to come with me.'

'What's up, Mrs. F.?'

'I'd like you to see something I found.'

The scythe was hanging in its proper place when we walked back into the barn. I showed Mort the shovel and the rag.

'I see what you mean,' he said. 'I've got some luminol in the car. Be right back.'

He returned wearing latex gloves and carrying a small canister of a chemical used by police to determine whether a stain, no matter how old or carefully cleaned, is blood. I'd seen it demonstrated before.

I closed the barn door, and Mort took the shovel and rag to the darkest corner. We waited a minute until our eyes had adjusted before Mort sprayed a tiny amount of the fluid on the shovel's handle and the rag. Almost immediately, the stains gave off a faint blue luminescence.

'It's blood, Mrs. F.,' he said. 'Of course, this is just a presumptive test. The forensic lab boys can be more specific. But looks like you came up with what might be the murder weapon. Judging from the wound on Ms. Swift's head, it could have been a shovel like this one that killed her.'

When we stepped outside, with Mort carrying the shovel and rag, I looked up at the main house, where Artie Sack stood in the driveway, his eyes trained on us. The moment he realized I'd seen him, he disappeared.

'If the blood on these things matches up with Matilda Swift's, I think I'm going to have to have a little talk with Artie Sack. These are the tools he uses, aren't they?'

'Yes, they are, but I can't conceive of Artie harming anyone.' I didn't mention that he'd not wanted me to go into the barn.

'But you never know about people, do you, Mrs. F.?'

'No, I suppose you don't.'

'Give you a ride back to town?' he asked, placing the shovel's blade and the rag in separate brown paper evidence bags, then putting them in the trunk of his marked car.

'I have my bike,' I said.

'Put it in the backseat,' he said, stripping off

138

his gloves.

'No, I'd better get on my way. Some errands to run and—no, on second thought, I think I will come with you.'

Mort looked at me and grinned. 'Can't resist, huh?'

'You might say that. Since I was the one who found the shovel and rag and discovered the bank statement for a safe-deposit box, I'd like to follow up with you.'

'No need to justify it to me, Mrs. F. Always a pleasure to have you on the case.'

# CHAPTER NINE

We stopped at the state police barracks just outside Cabot Cove to drop off the shovel and rag. 'Appreciate it if you fellas could dust this one and get them both to the lab as quick as possible to confirm there's blood on them,' Mort told the officer on duty. 'Presumptive test says there is, but could be some other chemical that reacts to luminol.'

'We'll get right on it, Mort,' the officer said. Our sheriff had forged a good relationship with the state police over the years, a positive situation when they had to work together solving crimes.

Wendell Watson was at the front desk when we walked into the sheriff's office.

'Anything new here, Wendell?' Mort asked as we headed down the hall.

Wendell followed. 'That Tremaine guy is raisin' hell in the back, Sheriff. He told me he was goin' to put a curse on me if I didn't let him out.'

'Did he now?' Mort said, laughing and tossing his tan Stetson on a couch in his cluttered office. 'What sort of curse?'

'He didn't say.'

'Maybe I'd better have a talk with him right now,' Mort said, 'before I have to let him go.'

'Oh,' Wendell said, remembering something. 'That lawyer, Joe Turco, was here. He says he's representin' Mr. Tremaine.'

'Turco's got that madman as a client?' Mort said. 'Thought he had better sense than that.'

'Mr. Turco says that if you don't release his client this afternoon, he'll sue you and everybody here.'

'Now that's a real curse, Wendell, having a lawyer on the case. Go bring Mr. Tremaine to the interview room.'

'Yes, sir.'

'Maybe I'd better leave,' I said.

'Don't see why, Mrs. F. Hang around. Maybe you've got some questions to ask our resident crazy.'

Tremaine was led into the small, spartan interview room at the rear of headquarters. He wore tight black jeans, a black T-shirt and leather sandals. His smug attitude of the night before had disappeared. His face was flushed with anger. When he saw me sitting at the table with Mort, I thought he might physically assault me. 'Why's she here?' he snapped at Mort.

'We haven't been formally introduced,' I said. 'I'm Jessica Fletcher.'

'Oh, so this is Jessica Fletcher, the world famous mystery writer,' Tremaine said. 'Doing research?' He plopped in a chair, crossed his legs and glared at me.

'Mrs. Fletcher's sort of a consultant to me and the department on this case, Mr. Tremaine.'

'Have you talked to my lawyer?' Tremaine asked.

'Heard he was in,' Mort said. 'Nice young fella.'

'I'll own this town if I am not released immediately,' Tremaine said. 'You have no reason to hold me this way. I didn't kill that crazy woman out at the Marshall estate, and I don't know a damn thing about it. You're persecuting me because of my beliefs.'

'Calm down, Mr. Tremaine,' Mort said. 'If you hadn't skipped out last night from Paul Marshall's house, you wouldn't be here now. You told me you crashed the party because you like parties. Where did you get the moose costume?'

'Boston.'

'Yeah, but how did you know the employees

141

would be wearing that costume?'

'One of Marshall-Scott Clothing's employees is a client of mine.'

'Client?'

'Comes to me for spiritual healing. She told me about the costumes and that they were being made in Boston. I ordered one.'

'Did you know the deceased?'

'The Swift woman? I knew all about her, knew she was evil.'

Mort glanced at me; I kept silent.

'She was evil, you say,' Mort said. 'Is that why you killed her?'

Tremaine guffawed. 'I didn't kill anybody, and you know it.'

Wendell knocked at the door, then opened it and said, 'Mr. Turco's here, Sheriff.'

Joe Turco pushed past Wendell and entered the room. 'Time to go,' he said to Tremaine, who stood.

'Hold on now, Mr. Turco,' Mort said. 'Your client and I have been having a pleasant chat.'

Turco looked at me. 'I didn't expect to see you here, Jessica.'

'I've just been sitting listening, Joe.'

Joseph Turco had moved to Cabot Cove from New York City, where he'd been a criminal and civil attorney. Tired of the big city's frenetic pace, he'd sought a more leisurely life; Cabot Cove seemed the perfect solution. He is a handsome young man with coal black hair and probing dark eyes, and he is an excellent attorney, I'd been told by those who'd employed him. His office is above Olde Tyme Floral, owned by close friends of mine, Beth and Peter Mullin, and I often find myself chatting with him when visiting the shop.

Turco turned to Mort. 'Are you charging my client with a crime, Mort—Sheriff?'

'Nope.'

'Then this friendly little chat is over.'

'Doesn't mean your client's off the hook,' Mort said. 'I'll be wanting to interview him again.'

'Just as long as I'm with him. Come on, Mr. Tremaine. Nice seeing you, Jessica.'

'Sign 'em out, Wendell,' Mort shouted down the hall.

When they were gone, Mort shook his head. 'The way I see it, Mrs. F., every day is Halloween when you're around that fruitcake.'

'He certainly works hard to be different.'

'I'd like to know more about Mr. Tremaine, but I don't figure I'm going to get much from him.'

'I think you're right,' I said, silently wondering how I might help. 'Are we going to the bank?'

He responded by asking his dispatcher, Marie Poutre, for the keys from the evidence room. She brought them in and laid them on the table.

I picked up the small one. 'Looks like a safe-deposit key to me,' I said.

'That it does. Well, let's head over and see if Doris will cooperate without a court order.'

\*       \*       \*

The Cabot Cove Savings Bank is situated in an old building just off the town square. The previous manager had retired after thirty years, his place taken by the assistant manager, Doris Sitar, a pretty, vivacious young woman who'd initiated a number of innovations, including free coffee and doughnuts. Charlene Sassi, owner of the town's prime bakery, objected, claiming that serving free doughnuts constituted unfair competition. Ms. Sitar solved the dilemma by serving only doughnuts purchased from Charlene's establishment. Most disputes in Cabot Cove are resolved through compromise and old-fashioned New England common sense.

'Howdy, Doris,' Mort said when we entered the bank and went to her desk.

'Hello, Sheriff, Jessica,' she said. 'To what do I owe this pleasure?'

'Here to ask you a favor,' Mort said. 'You heard about the murder last night at Paul Marshall's place?'

'I certainly did, heard it on the radio this morning. That's all people are talking about.'

'We understand Ms. Swift was a customer of the bank,' I said.

'Yes. She was in yesterday.' Doris

144

shuddered. 'It's scary to think of her being here alive in the afternoon, and dead that night.'

'What sort of business did she transact yesterday?' I asked.

Doris frowned. 'As I remember, she visited her safe-deposit box.'

'Which gets us to the reason we're here,' Mort said. He handed her the key found on Matilda Swift. 'Look like a key to one of your safe-deposit boxes?'

'Yes,' she said.

'This key was found on Ms. Swift's body last night, only we didn't realize what it was until today. I'd like to have a look inside that box.'

'It's been sealed,' Doris said. 'Automatic when there's been a death. The IRS.'

'Can't ever escape them, can we?' Mort said. 'Look, Doris, I'm not intending to take anything from the box. Just want to get a look at what she might have had in there. Of course, I can go to Judge Kaplan and get a court order, but I just figured you could save me the trouble.'

'I suppose there wouldn't be any harm in letting you see what's in it, Sheriff.'

'Now you know I like to be called Mort.'

Doris smiled. 'All right, Mort.' She summoned her assistant manager and asked him to accompany Mort to the safe-deposit vault, adding, 'The sheriff isn't taking anything from the box, just perusing what's in it.'

'Much obliged, Doris,' Mort said, following the assistant manager.

'You said Ms. Swift visited her safe-deposit box, Doris,' I said. 'Did you accompany her?'

'Yes. Did you know her, Jessica?'

'No, I didn't. I'd seen her a few times in town, but never had a conversation with her. Did she put something in the box?'

'I don't know. We give customers complete privacy. They take their box into a booth and close the door.'

'Of course.'

'I assume she removed something from it.'

'Oh?'

'When she handed the box back to me, I noticed that she held a plastic bag with some papers in it—you know, one of those Baggies from the kitchen. I didn't see that when she went into the booth.'

'A plastic bag? Why would she use a plastic bag? Was it full of papers?'

'Didn't seem to be, just a few documents. It was very flat and thin.'

'Uh-huh. How did she seem to you? Was she upset when she came in, worried, behave in any peculiar way?'

Doris smiled. 'I know this isn't very gracious, Jessica, but Ms. Swift was . . . well, she was an unusual lady.'

'Oh, I agree with that.'

'It was like there was a force surrounding her. Does that sound silly?'

'Not at all.'

'She had the strangest eyes.'

'Yes, I know.'

'She wasn't unpleasant, but I wouldn't call her friendly, either. Serious, very serious, and matter-of-fact.'

'Did she say anything to you? I mean, aside from asking to be taken to her safe-deposit box?'

'No. Oh, she did say something about Mr. Marshall's party.'

'What did she say about it?'

Doris screwed up her pretty face in thought. 'It was something about it being a bad night to have a party. No, what she said was, "Halloween is an *evil* night to have a party."'

'*Evil* night?'

'Yes, *evil* night.'

Mort returned with the assistant manager.

'Nothing, Mrs. F. Empty.'

'I'm not surprised.'

'You're not?'

'No. Thanks, Doris.'

'Yes, ma'am, thank you,' Mort said.

'My pleasure.' As she walked us through the bank lobby, Mort stopped at the refreshment table and plucked a powdered doughnut from a large tray. 'Charlene Sassi makes the best powdered doughnuts in Maine,' he said.

'No argument there,' Doris said. 'Any leads in the murder?'

'Afraid not,' Mort said.

'Well, at least the phones are finally fixed,' Doris said.

'You noticed that, too?' I asked.

'It's wonderful. It's the first day in weeks there hasn't been static on the line. I guess the repairmen found the problem.'

Mort and I looked at each other. 'I suppose so,' I said.

Mort tipped his Stetson. 'Thanks again, Doris.'

'My pleasure, Mort.'

We walked back to police headquarters a block away.

'Coming in?' Mort asked.

'No. You have Paul Marshall visiting this afternoon.'

'Wouldn't exactly call it a visit. I want to keep on the state boys about that shovel and rag. Have to call Doc Gillo, too, and see how his autopsy's coming along, check on Ms. Swift's blood type. If it is blood on that shovel and rag, and the type matches hers, we'll have something to work with.'

'Matching blood types won't prove it's her blood,' I said, 'just narrow the odds.'

'Right now,' he said, 'I'll take any lowering of the odds I can get. It'll help if the lab can pick up prints from that shovel.'

'If there are prints, Mort, they'll undoubtedly belong to Artie Sack. He's the one who uses the tools from that barn. I wore a pair of gardening gloves from there.'

'I'm sure you're right about that. Where are you headed, Mrs. F.?'

'Home for a bit. I thought I might drop by Paul Marshall's house later this afternoon, and I—'

'What?'

'I was thinking I'd like to get to know Lucas Tremaine a little better.'

'Can't imagine why.'

'For the same reason you said you'd like to know him better, to see whether he's capable of having killed Matilda Swift.'

'You leave that to me, Mrs. F.'

'Of course. Just thinking out loud. I'll call you later in the day.'


## CHAPTER TEN

I took a detour on my way home for a late lunch at Mara's. Friends asked me to join them at their tables, but I opted to eat alone in a corner booth, stopping on my way to grab a copy of that day's *Bangor Times*, a pile of which was always available for the luncheonette's patrons. The story of Matilda Swift's murder was on page three. As I read, I realized it would not have received as much attention as it did were it not for the scene of the crime, the palatial estate of Paul Marshall. Marshall had never run for public office, but

149

he was known as a force in Maine politics, a hefty contributor to candidates of his choice. The article mentioned, of course, that the murder had taken place during Marshall's annual Halloween bash, pointed out that all guests at the party were being questioned, and ended with a quote from Sheriff Mort Metzger:

We're in the preliminary phase of our investigation. My office and the state police are working closely together, and I'm confident we'll bring whoever committed this murder to justice in short order.

I silently hoped Mort was right, and read the rest of the paper while enjoying a filet of sole sandwich and cup of tea. Before leaving, I contemplated how to spend my afternoon. I'd told Mort I considered dropping by the Marshall house, although I didn't have a specific reason for doing so. It was just a hunch, but somehow I kept feeling that the key to this puzzle was still there on the estate—in the main house, cottages, the barn, perhaps even on the grounds.

As I pedaled along a country road, I tried to construct a mental list of those who might be considered primary suspects, assuming, of course, that the murderer wasn't a passer-by or someone from town with a grudge against Matilda.

Lucas Tremaine was my first candidate, but only because he was such a strange man. He had labeled Matilda 'evil,' which indicated to me that he possibly knew something about her, maybe even had some sort of a personal relationship with her.

She lived on the Marshall estate. That meant she'd probably come into contact with those living there more frequently than others in Cabot Cove, but they all seemed to deny knowing her. Paul Marshall? He'd said he was about to evict her. Jeremy Scott? No motive as far as I knew, which applied to Erica Marshall, too. Warren Wilson wasn't a resident of the estate, but was always around as Marshall's proverbial right-hand man. But again, no motive, unless he shared his boss's dislike of the victim.

Artie Sack? He was hard to fathom because of his mental impairment, but a sweeter-natured man I'd never met. Had Matilda Swift angered him to such an extent that he would strike her with . . .? I was now convinced the weapon was the shovel I'd found in the barn that morning.

And what about Robert Wandowski? His anger at Matilda the day of his daughter's late arrival from school was palpable, the temper he was capable of demonstrating unmistakable.

Such thoughts occupied me all the way to the Marshall property, and I was surprised

151

when I found myself already pedaling up the main driveway to the front of the house.

I leaned my bike against a tree and had started for the front door when angry voices stopped me. A leaded glass window to the right of the door was open; the sounds emanated from the room on the other side of it.

I stepped closer and cocked my head in the window's direction.

'We should have gone with him,' I heard a man say. He sounded like Warren Wilson, although I couldn't be sure.

'Paul didn't want us to.' I knew that was Jeremy Scott, no question about it.

Wilson: 'Damn it, we've got to be together in this. You're so pathetic, Jeremy. You do anything he says and—'

'Will the two of you shut up!' Erica Marshall speaking.

'Maybe if your father had come up with a formula that worked, we wouldn't be in this mess,' said Wilson.

'Don't you start about my father,' Jeremy growled. 'One more bad word about him and I'll—'

'You'll what, Jeremy, kill me, too?'

'You bastard!'

'Stop it!' Erica shouted; I sensed she'd had to step between them to head off a fight.

I debated whether to knock on the door. This obviously wasn't the right time to be visiting. As I pondered what to do, the sound of a car coming up the drive diverted my attention. It was Mort Metzger in his marked sheriff's car. With him was deputy Wendell Watson.

'Howdy, Mrs. F.,' Mort said as he exited the vehicle. 'Coming or going?'

'I was, uh, just leaving.'

Those inside the house had evidently heard the car, too, because the door opened and Erica Marshall stepped out onto the front brick patio. Behind her was Mrs. Sack, Artie's sister-in-law and the Marshall's housekeeper. Mort tipped his Stetson and approached them. 'Mrs. Sack, might Artie be inside with you?'

'No, he's not here. I think he's down working on one of the cottages, or in the barn.'

'Much obliged,' Mort said. He turned to Wendell: 'Let's go on down and find him.'

'Is Artie in some sort of trouble?' Mrs. Sack asked, her quivering voice mirroring her fear.

'Just got to ask him a few questions, ma'am,' Mort said over his shoulder as he and Wendell walked in the direction of the cemetery, Rose Cottage and the barn.

'Why does he want to talk to Artie?' Mrs. Sack asked me.

'I'm sure it's nothing to worry about,' I said, forcing lightness into my tone. 'Probably just routine.'

Erica disappeared inside, but Mrs. Sack remained in the open doorway until Mort and

Wendell, returned with Artie. 'I don't want to go to the police station,' Artie said. 'Oh, no, I don't want to go there.'

'Just want to get your fingerprints, Artie, and ask you a couple 'a questions,' Mort said. 'Have you back here for supper.'

'No, no, I don't want to go to the police station,' Artie repeated. 'Don't know nothing, don't know nothing, didn't do anything, didn't do anything.' The words came from him rapid-fire, like rounds from a machine gun.

'Now, don't make me have to force you,' Mort said, placing his hand reassuringly on Artie's shoulder. 'Get in the car with me and Wendell and let's get this over with.'

Foolishly, Artie turned to run, which necessitated Wendell grabbing him and pulling his arms behind his back. Artie whimpered and looked with wide, pleading eyes at his sister-in-law as Wendell guided him into the squad car's rear seat, holding a hand above Artie's head to keep it from bumping on his way in.

My heart went out to Artie and Mrs. Sack as Mort got behind the wheel, started the engine, and pulled away, Artie's face a mask of fright as he looked back at us through the rear window.

Jeremy Scott suddenly appeared in the doorway. 'Hello, Mrs. Fletcher,' he said, smiling. 'I didn't know you were here. Come on in, have some tea or a drink.'

'Thanks, Jeremy, but I have an appointment I have to get to.'

He frowned; I assumed he found it strange seeing me standing outside the house, having neither come from it nor having announced my arrival.

'But thanks for the invitation,' I said pleasantly, getting on my bike and rolling down the driveway to the street. I rode home as fast as I could, put the bike away in the garage, made myself a pot of tea and sat at the desk in my library.

The conversation among Erica, Jeremy and Warren kept coming back to me. I turned it over in my mind and made some notes on a pad. I wondered whether Mort had learned anything yet from the state police lab about the stains on Artie Sack's shovel and rag. The luminol had indicated it was blood. I had the uncomfortable feeling I was missing something.

Suddenly, I felt very tired. There had been so little sleep the night before. Added to that was the emotional trauma of being where someone had been brutally murdered, and spending my every waking moment since then thinking about that murder and who might have committed it.

I needed a day off. But I knew that wasn't in the cards until I'd gotten some answers as to why Matilda Swift had been murdered and, more important, who'd done it. This wasn't the first time I'd been gripped by such a compulsion, and probably wouldn't be the last. I could have, and probably should have, put it out of my mind and been content with getting updates from Mort Metzger and other investigators on the case.

But that wouldn't have been me, and if there's anything I've learned during my lifetime, it's the need to go with who you are, not who you'd prefer to be.

Richard Koser had taken multiple photographs at the party.

Not a bad place to start.

## CHAPTER ELEVEN

'Richard, are you in?' I called, rapping my knuckles on the door that stood ajar. The faint smell of darkroom chemicals drifted into my nostrils.

'C'mon in, I'm just finishing up,' came a disembodied voice. 'I'll be out in a moment.'

I left the door as I'd found it and wandered through Richard Koser's Craftsman-style bungalow to the kitchen in the back. My nose twitched. Here the chemical smell was augmented by something more exotic, spicy. Must be cumin, I thought, and onions, definitely onions. A man of many talents, Richard was not only a fine photographer, but also a masterful chef. He loved nothing more than poring through cookbooks and turning out exotic—and delicious—meals.

'Hi, Jessica,' Richard said, pulling aside a heavy curtain from the doorway to his darkroom. 'Can you stay for lunch? I'm trying out a new curry recipe for kooftah, and MaryJane went over to Bangor for the day.'

'I wish I could, Richard, but I'm supposed to meet Mort at his office, and I have a few errands to run before then. A rain check?'

'You've always got that,' he said, lifting the cover on a large pot and releasing a cloud of aromatic steam into the room. 'What can I do for you?'

'Well, I wondered if you'd had time to develop the photos you took at Paul Marshall's party.'

'You're in luck,' he said, replacing the pot cover after stirring the meatball stew. 'I just put them in the dryer—the photo dryer, that is—and they should be ready in a few minutes. If I can't talk you into kooftah, how about a cup of tea?'

'Tea would be lovely, thanks.'

'Green? Black? Herbal?'

'Whatever you're having will be fine.'

Richard took a white porcelain teapot from the shelf and put a kettle onto the stove after filling it with cold water. He was a purist, and I tried not to fidget as I seated myself at the kitchen table and waited impatiently for the

157

tea and photos to be ready.

As he fussed with cups and saucers and tea strainers, he questioned me about the murder investigation, which was, not surprisingly, now a topic of great speculation in Cabot Cove. 'Real shame about that lady. Mort's deputy— Harold, is it?—came to interview us yesterday, but we weren't any help. MaryJane and I were just having a good time at the party, not looking for murderers. Paul Marshall puts on quite a spread. Did they nail down when the murder took place?'

'The body was discovered after most of the guests had gone home, but I'm not sure what the time of death was.'

'The Lerners told us they were there when the body was found. Must have been pretty shocking, seeing the bloody victim and all. I suppose every party-goer will be getting a visit from the local constabulary.'

'I'm sure that's true.'

'Peculiar, isn't it, having a murder on Halloween, exactly a year after Tony Scott died in that fire? Paul Marshall's having a run of bad luck.'

'Seems to me Matilda Swift was the one with the bad luck,' I said, 'but, yes, the timing is ironic.'

'I heard that the nut over on the quarry road is one of the suspects. You heard that?'

'Lucas Tremaine? Mort hasn't said who he considers a suspect, but Mr. Tremaine was at the party, and an uninvited guest to boot. I'm not sure crashing a party qualifies as grounds for arrest, but it would be interesting to know what he's up to.'

'Well, if anyone can find out, Jessica, it would be you.'

'Thanks for your confidence, Richard, but I'm sure Mort and his people are doing a thorough job.'

'I just heard they hauled in Artie Sack. Don't they know Artie wouldn't hurt a fly, much less a person?'

'You've heard that already? Mort just took him in this afternoon.'

I wasn't sure how much of what I knew to share with Richard, or anyone else for that matter. But knowing the speed of Cabot Cove's grapevine, I decided it wouldn't hurt to preempt it, especially with a dear friend like Richard. After all, I was there seeking information from him—information possibly contained in photographs. But it wouldn't hurt to fudge a little.

'Mort brought Artie to headquarters to get his fingerprints, Richard. Just routine. If they find the murder weapon, they'll want everyone's prints.'

'The shovel?'

I sighed. 'Yes, the shovel. But it hasn't been established yet whether it was used to kill Matilda Swift.'

'I heard they found blood on it.'

'Oh I—'

'My money's on Tremaine,' he said, sparing my having to respond to whether blood had been found on the shovel. 'He's an oddball to begin with.'

The tea kettle whistled, and a buzzer sounded from the darkroom. I looked at Richard expectantly. He rinsed the teapot with boiling water from the kettle before carefully spooning in tea from a metal tin, then pouring more boiling water over the crushed leaves.

'The tea needs to steep a bit. I'll bring in the pictures for you to look at while we're waiting.' He disappeared behind the heavy curtain used to keep light from entering the darkroom when he was developing his work. He emerged with a box filled with warm photos, and a magnifying glass.

He set stacks of five-by-seven-inch pictures beside me and went to pour the tea. I was already sifting through the photos when he set a cup and saucer at my elbow and took a chair opposite me.

'What are you looking for exactly?' he asked, picking up a few photos I'd cast aside. 'I know it's not just my wonderful photography that has you tapping your foot like that.'

I laughed and sat back in my seat, reaching for the tea. 'You're right. I need to relax a bit. This murder case has me up nights worrying if I've missed anything.'

'And have you?'

'That's what I'm trying to figure out. I'd love to see a picture of the murderer with a big sign saying "I did it." Failing that, I thought the photos might stimulate some ideas, or indicate . . . something.'

I sighed and sipped my tea. 'Are these all the photos from that night?'

'You've got six rolls of film there, Jessica. Should keep you occupied for a bit.'

'Do you mind if I sit here and look through them?'

'Not at all,' he replied, getting up and turning off the flame under the kooftah, 'as long as you don't mind if I get on with my work. I've got more film to develop, but not from the party.'

'Don't let me keep you. I'll just study these a while and call out when I leave.'

Richard re-entered his darkroom, and I arranged the photos into three piles—those I hadn't looked at yet, those I'd seen and wanted to look at again and those I didn't need to re-examine.

A half hour and 216 pictures later, I rubbed my tired eyes, strained from squinting through the magnifier and staring at the myriad images of masked and moose guests cavorting at the Marshall party. Richard was a wonderful photographer, and it was hard not to allow the overall impression of his pictures to interfere with my concentration on the details. But at last I'd gotten my look-at-again pile down to three photographs. One shot was of the moose couple dancing, with other guests observing them. Their grace, despite the awkward costumes, had drawn admiring attention.

Another picture showed Paul Marshall standing on the central staircase of his manor house, addressing the assembled multitude.

The third, taken on the patio, showed guests sitting on the brick wall overlooking the back lawn. I examined them again, searching the figures in the background. I felt a prickle on the back of my neck. There was something here. What was it? Raising the magnifying glass again, I pored over the photo of Paul Marshall. Though Richard had taken several shots of the scene, the angle of this particular photo was slightly to Marshall's left, and caught the side of the staircase as well as a glimpse into the dining room. There, mostly hidden by pirates and witches and cheerleaders and soldiers and cowgirls, was someone who wasn't supposed to be there. Her arms were raised as she was about to replace the moose head she'd taken off. It was Lauren Wandowski.

Richard emerged from the darkroom. 'See any you'd like, Jess? I'll make you up some prints.'

'Just this one,' I said, indicating the one with Lauren.

'Why that one?'

'Nothing special, Richard. Lauren wasn't

supposed to have been at the party but—'
Whatever I said would be grist for
conversation around town the next day. I
kissed him on the cheek. 'Thanks, Richard. I'll
tell you all about it next time I see you. Have
to run.'

'Before you go,' he said, 'take a look at
these.' He held up eight-by-ten prints that
were still wet from processing.

'What are they?' I asked.

'I was around town a few days ago shooting
stuff for my architectural series. I'm still
working on that book I told you about, vintage
buildings of New England.'

'The book's a great idea, Richard, only I
don't see any houses of particular historic
interest in these shots.'

'I know. There aren't any. While I was
wandering around, I saw the deceased.'

'Ms. Swift?'

'Yeah. She's intrigued me ever since she
moved to Cabot Cove. Strange-looking lady,
I'm sure you'll agree. Anyway, I had a long
lens on my camera and snuck a couple of shots
of her—without her knowing, of course.'

I leaned closer to the prints and narrowed
my eyes. 'Is that her?' I asked.

'Yeah.'

'What happened? Was your camera
malfunctioning?'

'No. It was working fine.'

'But she's out of focus.'

'And everything else is in focus,' he said.

'It's as though there's a mist surrounding her, gauze, like the way they used to photograph fading movie queens through lenses smeared with Vaseline.'

'I know,' he said. 'Beats me why these shots came out this way.'

'Well, there's got to be a tangible explanation for it, a physical reason.'

We looked at each other, and I wondered whether he was thinking what I was thinking. He satisfied my curiosity. 'Maybe she's The Legend, Jess,' he said, laughing.

I didn't laugh.

\*　　　\*　　　\*

No one seemed to be at home at the Wandowski cottage when I arrived and leaned my bike against the gate, but then I heard a child's voice coming from the wooded area at the side of the house. A moment later, Lauren and her daughter, Julie, emerged from the trees, the child swinging her lunchbox and chattering animatedly. Both saw me at the same time. Lauren looked worried, but Julie raced to me and sang out, 'Hi! You're the lady who came here with the policemen, right?' She stopped in front of me and her smile faded as she remembered that day. 'My mom told me Mrs. Swift died. She was a nice lady. Did you like her? Daddy didn't like her. But she was

164

nice to me. She let me bake cookies with her.'

'I'm afraid I didn't know her very well,' I said, smiling at the child's unbridled enthusiasm. Lauren was approaching, so I quickly asked, 'Who else was baking cookies with you when you visited Mrs. Swift, Julie?'

'The pretty lady from the big house was there, but she didn't help much. I did all the mixing,' she piped up proudly.

'That's enough, Julie,' her mother said, reaching for her daughter's shoulders and turning her toward the cottage. 'I'm sure Mrs. Fletcher has more important things to discuss. You go on in.' She gave her a little push. 'Take a snack. I'll be right there.'

Lauren looked ill at ease. 'I wasn't expecting company . . .' She trailed off, her eyes following Julie, who waved at me as she opened the cottage door and slipped inside.

'I won't keep you long,' I said, handing Lauren the photo Richard had given me. 'Your husband said you didn't attend the party, but I'm pretty sure that's you.' My finger pointed to the corner of the picture.

Lauren's face became red, and she stammered as she handed the picture back. 'Bob, uh, I mean . . . what I mean is we couldn't get anyone to stay with Julie, so we took turns at the party.'

'Why would your husband lie to Sheriff Metzger about that?'

'Oh, God.' Her eyes filled with tears. 'I told

165

him we'd get in trouble. He didn't want the sheriff to know he'd left the party to allow me to come because . . .'

'Because that would have given him the opportunity while he was away from the party to kill her. He did threaten Ms. Swift the day your daughter was with her, Mrs. Wandowski.'

'I know he did, but he didn't kill her, Mrs. Fletcher. I know my husband. He has a temper at times, but he could never kill anyone. Oh, my God,' she wailed. 'How could this have happened to us? Are you going to have him arrested? He's innocent. I know he's innocent.'

I wasn't sure of Robert Wandowski's innocence, but I didn't want to further upset his wife. 'Why don't you have Bob tell the sheriff the truth,' I said. 'It will be much better if it comes from him.'

She wiped tears from beneath her eyes and nodded stiffly. 'I'll do that. I promise. I'll have him go straight to the sheriff's office when he gets home from work.'

She backed toward the cottage while I went to where I'd left my bicycle. 'I promise,' she called out from the doorway as I got on the bike and rode away, looking back over my shoulder to see Julie Wandowski's little face in the window.

*     *     *

The sheriff's office sounded like a big city

police station when I walked in the next morning. Phones were ringing nonstop, and Wendell, Harold and Marie were all talking at once. With her hand on one still-ringing phone, Marie rested the receiver of another on her shoulder and said to me above the hullabaloo, 'Mort had to go down to the state police barracks to pick up the lab report on Matilda Swift. A tanker truck overturned down on the highway—a big oil spill—and the press is calling about the Swift investigation.'

'Did the blood type match Ms. Swift's?' I asked.

Marie nodded.

'Can I help?' I asked.

'You can pick up any ringing phone. Just take a message and one of us will call back.'

I grabbed a pad and pen from the nearest desk, seated myself in a rolling chair and answered a phone with, 'Cabot Cove Sheriff's Office.'

'This is George Walker. Is Sheriff Metzger there, please?'

'I'm sorry, the sheriff is out of the office at the moment. May I take a message for him?' I asked, writing down his name.

'Yes, ma'am, you may. I'm with the United Insurance Company in Salem, Massachusetts. The sheriff called me about one of our clients, Matilda Swift. Ms. Swift had a life insurance policy with us, and I understand she has passed away.'

167

My heart started beating quickly. 'Yes,' I said.

'That reminds me, I've got to call her lawyer. Do you need his name?'

'Yes, the sheriff will need that.'

'His name is Stuart Shippee. He's here in Salem, too.' He gave me the lawyer's phone number.

I wrote down the information, then asked, 'Mr. Walker, did the sheriff leave word what other information he needed from you?'

'Not specifically, Officer, but I assume he'll want to know the name of the beneficiary and the amount of the death benefit.'

I stalled for a moment, debating whether or not to correct his impression that he was speaking with a police officer. He took my hesitation to mean I was waiting for the answer.

'Let me see,' he said. 'I believe the amount of the policy is five hundred . . .' I heard him shuffle some papers. 'Thousand. Yes, five hundred thousand.'

I let out a breath. Matilda Swift may not have lived as modest a life as I'd originally imagined.

'And the beneficiary?' I coaxed.

'The beneficiary is her nephew in California. I'm not sure the address is current, but his name is Scott something. No, that's not right.' I heard him turn a page. 'Here it is. That's his last name. Scott. The beneficiary is Jeremy Scott.'

168

# CHAPTER TWELVE

I called the number for the attorney, Stuart Shippee, which Matilda Swift's insurance agent had given me, and was surprised when he picked up personally on the first ring.

'Hello?' he said in a voice that told me he was an elderly gentleman.

'Mr. Shippee?'

'Yes?'

'My name is Jessica Fletcher. I'm calling from Cabot Cove, Maine.'

'Oh?'

'I was given your name and number by George Walker, an insurance agent for a Matilda Swift. Unfortunately, Ms. Swift died recently. I was told you were her attorney.'

'Yes, that's correct. She died, you say?'

'Yes. She was murdered.'

'Oh, my.'

'Mr. Walker told me that Ms. Swift's beneficiary on her life policy was someone named Jeremy Scott.'

'Yes?'

'Is that true?'

'I wouldn't know. I put Matilda in touch with George because she needed a life insurance policy. I wasn't involved in writing the policy. You say she was murdered?'

'Yes. The day before yesterday.'

His sigh was long and deep. 'Oh, my,' he said again. 'Has the murderer been apprehended?'

'I'm afraid not. Mr. Shippee, I was wondering whether—'

'What did you say your name was?'

'My name? Jessica Fletcher.'

'The mystery writer?'

'Yes.'

'Oh, my. This is indeed a pleasure, Mrs. Fletcher. I've read every one of your books. I've been a lover of murder mysteries for many years.'

'I'm pleased to hear that, Mr. Shippee. It's always nice speaking with someone who's read my books.'

What I didn't bargain for was that this nice man was such a fan of murder mysteries that he consumed the next fifteen minutes discussing the relative merits of mystery writers. He was partial to the British—P. D. James, Ruth Rendell, Agatha Christie and Dorothy Sayers, although he admitted to a fondness for the American hard-boiled Chandler and Hammett, as well as a variety of recent best-selling writers, including me. He spent a few minutes analyzing my strengths and weaknesses as a writer before allowing me to return to the reason for my call.

'Mr Shippee,' I said, 'did Matilda Swift leave a will?'

'Oh, yes, of course.'

'I realize it hasn't been probated yet, but I wonder if you could tell me who the heir to her estate is.'

'I believe that wouldn't be out of order, Mrs. Fletcher. Do you prefer the cozy brand of mystery, or the police procedural?'

'Ah . . . let me think about that, Mr. Shippee, while you look up Matilda Swift's heir.'

'Yes, of course.'

I heard him humming, and opening and shutting drawers. He came back on the line and said, 'Here we are, Mrs. Fletcher. Yes, I remember my conversation with Ms. Swift when we drew up the document. She said she didn't have any close family. There was a brother, I think, but he'd died in some sort of industrial accident shortly before she came to me for a will.'

'That would have been shortly after Halloween of last year,' I said.

'November. Yes, that would be after Halloween. She said she would have left her estate to her brother had he lived but—well, we can't always have things go the way we would like them to go, can we?'

'No.'

'Her brother had a son, she mentioned, her nephew. She'd never met him, but wanted to leave what she had to him. He lived somewhere in California. She wasn't sure where.'

'And his name is Jeremy Scott.'

171

'You are absolutely right, Mrs. Fletcher. An impressive demonstration of deductive powers. Do you know this young man, have an idea where he might be found?'

'I'm not sure, Mr. Shippee, but I believe I'll be able to find out for you very quickly.'

'That would be appreciated. Do you know of Ms. Swift's burial plans? I'll need an official death certificate to begin the probate process.'

'Because her death was a murder, Mr. Shippee, her body won't be released for some time.'

'To be expected. Will you be visiting Salem, Mrs. Fletcher? I would enjoy sitting down together and discussing the current state of the murder mystery with you.'

'No immediate plans, Mr. Shippee, but if I ever do get to Salem, I'll look you up.'

'That would be wonderful, a great pleasure for me. Good day, Mrs. Fletcher. Thank you for calling.'

That confirmed it. Jeremy Scott was Matilda Swift's nephew, which made his father, Tony, her brother. I sat back and formulated questions.

Did Jeremy know Matilda was his aunt? Probably not originally, since the attorney, Shippee, indicated that Matilda claimed never to have met her nephew. But did she know Jeremy was in Cabot Cove when she elected to move here? If so, had she told him who she was once she arrived?

It couldn't have been a coincidence that Matilda Swift rented the Rose Cottage on the Marshall estate, the same cottage that her brother, Anthony Scott, had occupied until his death. Or was it?

Matilda had drawn up her will shortly after Tony Scott died in the fire at his lab. Obviously, she knew of his death. Who had told her? Had she read it in the papers? It wasn't likely that Scott's demise would have been news in Salem, Massachusetts.

The best source for at least some of the answers was Jeremy Scott. I was tempted to pick up the phone, call Jeremy and ask him outright. But I held back on that urge.

Instead, I called Richard Koser at his home office. Besides his involvement in photography and gourmet cooking, he could be generally found hunched in front of an elaborate computer system.

'Richard, it's Jessica. Can I bother you again?'

'You're never a bother. What's up?'

'A technical question from a distinctly non-technical person. Would the U.S. Trademark and Patent Office have a website on the Internet?'

'Sure. Everybody else does. Why?'

'Mind if I pop over?'

'Not at all.'

*     *     *

173

I sat with Richard in front of his large-screen monitor and watched him access the Internet, then go to the home page, as it's called, for the Trademark and Patent Office.

'What do you want me to look up, Jess?'

'I'd like to see whether anyone has applied for a patent on BarrierCloth.'

'Tony Scott's invention?'

'Yes.'

'I thought he failed to come up with a working formula.'

'That's what everyone says, Richard, but I'm just curious—the writer in me.'

'Well, let's take a look.'

It took a minute for him to bring up the information I sought.

'That's interesting,' he said.

'Yes, isn't it? Can you print it out for me?'

'Sure thing. I suppose this means Tony did perfect the formula and had it patented in the company's name.'

'Not necessarily,' I said.

'Why not?'

As the pages slowly emerged from his printer, I said, 'First, Richard, according to this, the application for a patent on BarrierCloth wasn't filed in the name of Marshall-Scott Clothing. Look. It's been filed by another company, Nutmeg Associates, Inc.'

'Must be a subsidiary of Marshall-Scott Clothing. They have a couple of them, I know, because I did some photography for one of them earlier this year.'

'You're probably right,' I said. 'But as for Tony Scott having perfected the formula, there's nothing to say that the formula submitted to the Patent and Trademark Office actually works. Here, look at this note on the status of the patent:

Patent pending independent testing for flammability. Documentation to be submitted by Excel Laboratory, Burlington, Vermont.

'Wasn't flammability always the problem?'

'As far as I know. I wonder how the tests came out.'

'Assuming they've been completed,' Richard said, chewing his cheek. 'Mind if I ask you a question, Jess?'

'Of course not.'

'Obviously, your interest is more than simply being a murder mystery writer. What are you really looking for?'

'I wish I knew, Richard.' I took another close look at the printout in my hands. 'Do you see the date that this patent was applied for?'

'November sixteenth, a year ago. It says it'll probably be another year, especially with those tests going on in Vermont. These government agencies move slow as molasses.'

'November sixteenth, a couple of weeks

after Tony Scott died in that tragic fire. Richard, you're a doll.'

'Glad to help, but I wish I knew where this was leading you, Jess.'

'I do, too, but if I ever figure it out, you'll be among the first to know.'

## CHAPTER THIRTEEN

'Good morning,' I said to Beth Mullin as I entered Olde Tyme Floral, in the center of town.

'Hello, Jessica. Out for a constitutional?'

'You might say that.'

Beth's husband, Peter, called a greeting from the rear of the shop, where he was preparing a floral delivery. I waved back.

'Is Joe Turco upstairs?' I asked, referring to the young attorney who'd taken on Lucas Tremaine as a client.

'I think so. Saw him come in about an hour ago.'

'Well, think I'll pop up and see if he—'

I was saved a trip upstairs when Turco burst through the door to the flower shop, cradling a bundle of papers, and looking very much like someone in a hurry.

'I was just coming up to see you,' I said.

'Have to be another time, Jessica. I'm off to a meeting with everyone's favorite person and my most recent client.'

'You really are representing Tremaine?' Peter Mullin asked, coming from the back room to join the conversation.

Turco shook his head and exhaled loudly. 'Yes, I am representing Lucas Tremaine because . . . because he needs a lawyer and I happen to be a lawyer, who, I might add, believes that everyone deserves legal representation when they're in trouble with the law, especially somebody like Tremaine who's being persecuted for being different and controversial.'

'Is he in trouble with the law?' Beth asked. 'Is he the prime suspect in the murder of that woman out at Paul Marshall's place?'

'He's a suspect,' Turco said, 'like everyone else who was at the party. Look, I'd love to discuss this with you, but I'm already late for my meeting. I need some flowers sent to my sister in New York. Her birthday today.' He handed Beth a business card; he'd written his sister's name, address and phone number on the back. 'A nice colorful arrangement,' he said. 'Keep it under fifty bucks, okay? I'll pay you when I get back.'

I followed him past the door to the street. 'Joe, a quick question.'

'Huh? Sure. What?'

'Have you heard of a corporation called Nutmeg Associates?'

'No. Why?'

'I was thinking of buying stock in it. I think it's a subsidiary of Marshall-Scott Clothing.'

He shrugged. 'Never heard of it, but I'll check some sources when I get back.'

'That's great, Joe. Thanks.'

During my brief conversation with Joe Turco, Brenda Brody, *Cabot Cove Magazine*'s copy editor, entered Olde Tyme Floral. I followed her inside.

' 'Morning, Brenda,' I said.

She looked at me with what I can only label an angry expression.

'How are things at the magazine?' I asked.

'Just fine,' she replied. She placed an order with Beth for two bouquets of flowers to be delivered later that day to Lucas Tremaine's building on the old quarry road.

'Special occasion?' I asked.

'Our weekly meeting, calling to the spirits. Lucas likes to have flowers at the séance.'

'Oh? Sounds like a good idea,' I said.

Brenda, a short, compact woman with red hair and very thick glasses, completed her transaction and turned to leave. She reached the door, stopped, faced me and said, 'You know, Jessica, for a writer you're a very close-minded woman.'

'I'm sorry you feel that way,' I said.

'I suppose because you're very successful and famous, you feel justified in dismissing what you don't understand.'

'Such as Lucas Tremaine's activities?'

'Exactly. Being skeptical, even scornful of what he does when you don't even *know* what he does strikes me as prejudiced—something I'd never known you to be.'

'Maybe you're, right, Brenda. I don't know what Mr. Tremaine does.'

'*Dr.* Tremaine.'

'I didn't realize he had a doctoral degree. It just seems to me that paying money to be put in touch with a departed loved one doesn't—' I shook my head. 'Well, I have to admit, it doesn't make any sense to me.' She started to respond, but I held up a hand. 'Then again,' I said, 'I've never attended a séance, so I agree with you. I shouldn't be scornful of something I don't know about.'

'That's nice to hear,' she said.

'What happens at one of his séances, Brenda? Educate me.'

'Are you really interested in knowing?'

'I wasn't until we started talking. But, as you say, if I'm going to judge Mr. Tremaine—Dr. Tremaine—I should know what I'm talking about.

Brenda started to explain, step-by-step, what happens at a séance, but stopped after a minute and said, 'I have a better idea. Why don't you come with me tonight?'

'Come with you? Me? Go to a séance?'

'Yes. That way you can see for yourself.'

'I don't know, Brenda, I—'

'Lucas could try to put you in touch with

179

Frank.'

The mention of my deceased husband stung for a moment, particularly in the context of trying to communicate with him through the mumbo jumbo of a séance conducted by a charlatan. But two things immediately crossed my mind. I had wanted to learn more about Lucas Tremaine in connection with Matilda Swift's murder—and I did not want to continue being known as someone who's critical of others without actually knowing what they do, and how they do it.

'All right,' I said. 'What time?'

'Nine. Want me to pick you up?'

'I'd appreciate that,' I said. 'I don't drive, as you know.'

'You really should learn, Jessica,' Brenda said.

I smiled. 'You're right about that, Brenda. One of these days.'

'I'll pick you up at eight-thirty,' she said.

'And I'll be waiting.'

When she was gone, Beth Mullin looked up from an arrangement she was creating and said, 'You're really going to a Lucas Tremaine séance, Jess?'

'Looks like it.'

'Never thought I'd see that,' she said, artistically placing gorgeous pink roses into the arrangement.

'I never thought I would, either. Next thing you know, I'll be learning to drive a car.'

# CHAPTER FOURTEEN

From a distance, the old roadhouse looked dark when Brenda and I drove down the old quarry road that evening. But as we neared the dilapidated building, I could detect the flicker of candlelight through a downstairs window. A half dozen cars were pulled up onto the property, parked in haphazard fashion on the mostly dirt lawn, as if their drivers had been too rushed to consider parking in neat rows. I wasn't even sure all of the cars were functional; some may have belonged to the previous owners of the building and been left to rust as a grim reflection of the aging structure.

Brenda found a vacant area away from the other vehicles and shut off the engine. She lowered her head for a moment, as if in prayer, then looked at me. 'Are you ready?' she whispered.

'Yes, but why are you whispering?'

'Lucas likes us to spend some quiet time before we come in. If we're peaceful and quiet, our souls will be open to the spirits around us. He says loud noise discourages them.'

As we and others exited our vehicles, the thuds of car doors being closed filled the night, and I wondered if we were chasing away the spirits before we even started.

I looked up into the black sky, the scrim for a full moon and millions of stars. We have spectacular night skies in Maine, crystal clear and often startling in intensity. I was glad for the light the moon generated. Without it, we would have been shrouded in darkness as we approached the front of the crumbling building, the candle in the window the only illumination.

Brenda opened the front door, exposing a small anteroom. On a table on the wall opposite the door was a large glass globe containing a blue bulb that washed the wall with azure light. The odor of incense reached me as I went up three rickety wooden steps and entered the anteroom. Other than the faint dissonant tinkling of wind chimes, there was silence inside the building—until a gust of wind slammed the door shut behind me. Brenda, myself and two others who'd just come in jumped at the sudden loud sound.

I leaned to Brenda's ear. 'What do we do now? Where do we go?'

She answered by nodding in the direction of a pair of large double doors to our right. I followed her as she opened one and we stepped through. We were now in a larger room lighted by candles in wall sconces high on either side. As my eyes acclimatized to the dimness, I saw that we were in a chapel of sorts. A makeshift altar on which two candles burned brightly took up the far end. The smell of incense was strong. I looked for pews; there weren't any. Instead, the middle of the room had a large round table surrounded by a dozen chairs, some already occupied.

Brenda seemed transfixed by the very act of being there. 'Brenda,' I said.

She snapped out of her reverie and looked at me as though I were a stranger.

'Should we sit down?' I asked in a whisper.

'Yes,' she answered.

We took two vacant chairs at a side of the table that had us facing the altar. Others at the table had their heads bowed, their hands flat on the tabletop. I saw Brenda assume that position, and I did the same. With my eyes closed, and the tinkling of the wind chimes the only sound, a lovely calm came over me, as though my brain had been emptied of all clutter, leaving it free to dwell only on tranquil thoughts, pleasant thoughts, light and airy images of blue skies, green pastures and colorful birds in flight.

But that reverie was interrupted by a pin-spot that suddenly came to life from above the table, bathing its center in white light. Then a man's voice said, 'Good evening.'

Lucas Tremaine walked slowly toward us from the direction of the altar, his figure silhouetted against the candlelight there. He wore some sort of billowing gown that fluttered behind him as he approached. When he reached the table, I could see that his gown, more a cape actually, was purple, and covered him from neck to ankle.

'Good evening, Dr. Tremaine,' his supplicants said reverentially, and in unison, the effect of their combined monodic voices like a Gregorian chant.

Eleven of the twelve chairs were occupied. Before taking the remaining empty one, a large red leather chair with a high back, Tremaine placed in the center of the table an object he was carrying. It looked to me like a crystal ball of the sort fictional fortune-tellers seem always to have in front of them. The overhead pin-spot caught its glossy surface, and was reflected back in myriad colors that moved and made the luminous orb seem alive.

'I'd like to welcome a newcomer to our group, Jessica Fletcher. I'm sure most of you know her as a famous writer of murder mysteries.'

Those at the table glanced at me but said nothing. I didn't know whether he'd recognized me when he arrived at the table, or if Brenda had alerted him earlier that I'd be there. Either way, I hadn't a clue whether it was appropriate at a séance to respond, so I said nothing, nor did Tremaine seem to expect a response. He sat back and closed his eyes; his lips trembled, or he might have been chanting things to himself, his mouth silently forming the words. He opened his eyes, took in each of us at the table, then asked, 'Who wishes to speak with a loved one who has crossed the divide into the next dimension?'

People shifted in their seats; were they being polite and waiting for others to go first, or were they unsure whether they wanted to jump over the 'divide,' as Tremaine called it?

Finally, Brenda Brody spoke: 'I want to speak with Russell,' she said, her voice quivering. 'I need to hear from him whether he was ever unfaithful to me. There were rumors that still keep me awake at night, torture me every day. I want to ask him directly so I can find some peace.'

I thought of the Legend of Cabot Cove and of her husband's infidelity, which led to his ax murder and her suicide. It seemed to me that Brenda had nothing to gain and so much to lose by attempting to find out whether her husband had been faithful. Of course, it was an academic exercise, I knew. No one, including Lucas Tremaine, was going to put Brenda in touch with Russell, no matter how much she paid. I watched and listened as Tremaine went to work.

'Please join hands,' he told us. I reached left and right and grasped the hands of the people next to me, one of them Brenda. In the ensuing silence, I stared into the crystal ball on the table; its reflected light played on everyone's faces and the table itself. The heavy scent of incense was everywhere. The effect was mesmerizing, and I felt myself being drawn into the ball, wanting to enter it and revel in its brilliance.

Brenda's hand squeezed mine tightly, and her breathing became deep and labored. I found myself fighting to remain alert to what was happening. I was both witness to the scene and participant, watching it with detachment, yet feeling the emotions of the moment.

Tremaine started talking: 'The collective force of those gathered here tonight is reaching out to Russell Brody on behalf of his loyal and loving wife, Brenda . . . We are all friends who share a common soul, a mutual love for Brenda and her dearly departed husband of many years, Russell . . .'

As he continued to call out for Russell to make an appearance, I looked around the table. I was the only one whose eyes weren't shut tight. My companions murmured sounds that were only that—sounds, not words.

I began to feel hot and light-headed. Tremaine's voice had become a monotone, a drone, threatening to put me to sleep.

'. . . we beseech you, Russell Brody, to join us. Speak with your living wife, answer the question that torments her day and night, allow her to—'

Brenda suddenly stiffened in her chair, yanked her hand free of mine and gasped. Everyone looked to her, including me. She looked up into the pin-spot above, and her round, freckled face broke into a joyous smile.

186

'Russell, Russell,' she said, lifting her arms to him. 'I see you, Russell. Yes, I hear you fine. How are you? I miss you so much.'

I strained to see what she was seeing and hear what she was hearing, but I was unsuccessful. All I could do was what the others were doing—watch Brenda and wait for something else to happen.

Brenda conversed with her dead husband for a minute or two, as though they were seated in their kitchen, chatting over a cup of coffee: 'Are you taking care of yourself, Russell? Do you have what you need? Have you met any of our friends yet?'

Then she closed her eyes, moaned and said, 'He's leaving me, he's fading. Russell, Russell, please tell me, were you ever unfaithful when we were married?'

She shuddered, then slumped back in her chair, and when she lifted her head, her face was glowing. 'He was faithful to me.' She turned to Tremaine. 'Oh, Dr. Tremaine, you are wonderful. How can I ever thank you?'

'It warms my heart to be able to play a role in uniting you with Russell,' he said in soft, measured tones.

Tremaine then looked at me. 'Mrs. Fletcher, is there a question you'd like to ask Frank?'

'How do you know my dead husband's name?' I asked, my voice betraying the shock of hearing Frank's name come from Tremaine.

'I know a lot of things, Mrs. Fletcher. Would you like to talk to Frank? I believe I can help you do that.'

I was dizzy from the incense, and had had enough of this nonsense. Brenda's assurances from Russell were surely wish fulfillment, and I no longer wanted to participate in this charade. I stood. 'No, thank you,' I said, straightening my skirt.

'The séance isn't over,' Brenda said.

'Please go on without me,' I said. 'Is there a phone, Mr. Tremaine?'

'Of course.'

He got up and excused himself, then went with me to his office off the lobby. He snapped on the overhead light and pointed to the phone. 'Be my guest,' he said pleasantly. 'Need a taxi?'

'No I . . .'

'You really hate me, don't you?'

'No, Mr. Tremaine, I don't hate you, but I think it's unconscionable that you take money from these people who are grieving. How much will Brenda pay you tonight for allegedly putting her in touch with her husband?'

'Two hundred dollars.'

'Not a bad payday for a night's work, if everyone in there elects to make contact with a deceased loved one.'

'Mrs. Fletcher, you're an intelligent woman. I'm sure in researching your many novels you've done some looking into the human mind and human behavior.'

'Of course I have.'

'You are aware, of course, of the potency of suggestion with certain people.'

'Yes.'

'Some people are more suggestible than others. They're the ones who are more easily hypnotized. Mrs. Brody is one of those people.'

'Are you admitting she didn't have a conversation with her husband, that she was hypnotized in some way, was a victim of the power of suggestion, *your* suggestion?'

'All I'm saying, Mrs. Fletcher, is that whether she actually did talk to him or not tonight, she'll sleep a lot better from now on, believing he didn't cheat on her during their long marriage. I'd say I've done a very nice thing tonight for her. At two hundred bucks, it's a medical bargain.'

'I understand what you're saying, but— excuse me, I will use the phone.'

I dialed Seth Hazlitt's number.

'Did I wake you?' I asked when he answered sleepily.

'Just dozing in the chair, Jessica.'

'Seth, would you be a dear and pick me up?'

'Where are you?'

'Out on the old quarry road, at the building Lucas Tremaine uses.'

'What? What are you doing there with that madman?'

189

'I'll explain it when I see you. I'm quite safe. There are ten other people with me.'

Tremaine laughed from behind me.

'Sit tight, Jessica,' Seth said. 'I'll be there in a couple 'a minutes.'

'Of course you're safe,' Tremaine said after I'd hung up. 'I'm really quite harmless, unless you think I murdered that crazy lady out at the Marshall place.'

'Crazy?' I said. 'She might have been a little odd, but I saw nothing to indicate she was mentally unbalanced—"crazy," as you put it.'

'You may be a sophisticated woman, Mrs. Fletcher, and a successful writer of best-selling books, but there's a great deal you evidently don't understand.'

'I won't deny that,' I said. 'I assume you're referring to the world you inhabit, the so-called spirit world.'

'Exactly. It exists, Mrs. Fletcher, as surely as we exist in this tangible world. Are you one of those people who has to touch, see and feel something before you can accept it?'

'Yes, except I also am open enough not to summarily dismiss what other people believe, even though it's not part of my experience.'

He clapped his hands. 'Aha,' he said. 'I'm making progress. Matilda Swift was not of this world, you know. Can you accept *that*?'

'No.'

I remembered back to seeing Matilda's image in Richard Koser's photographs, ethereal and blurred, as though surrounded by a force beyond the ability of the camera to record.

'Suit yourself,' he said. 'Most people would respond as you do. That's why the world needs people like me. I have an insight into those like Matilda Swift. I understand them because I am one with them.'

I wanted to say 'rubbish' but didn't. Instead, I ignored his comment and idly picked up a small device next to the phone. It was a narrow silver tube with an opening on one end and a ring at the other.

'Please don't feel you have to stay here with me,' I said. 'My ride will be along in a minute.'

'It's no trouble.'

'What's that?' I pointed to a wire leading out the top of a window. As Tremaine looked to where I pointed, I pocketed the silver tube.

'It's a public address system that I've set up for outdoor meetings in the spring.'

'For when your followers can no longer squeeze around a table?'

He didn't say anything in return, but his face changed. At first, I thought he'd become angry. Then I realized he was going into some sort of a self-induced trance. His eyes rolled high into his head, revealing mostly white beneath them, and he wrapped his arms about himself and shuddered.

'Are you all right?' I asked.

He held up a hand. 'Shh.'

I watched as he squeezed his eyes shut tight, opened them, trained them on me and said, 'The Legend is coming, Jessica Fletcher. You may not believe, but she will be here. I see . . . I see roses, hundreds of roses on a long brick wall . . . She has . . . she has answers for why Matilda Swift was killed . . . she will appear . . . appear . . . two nights from now . . .'

He slowly sank to the floor on his knees. He was silent for a long time.

'Mr. Tremaine, are you—?'

He looked up at me and grinned, then stood and brushed off his purple robe. 'Sorry,' he said, 'but sometimes visions come to me at the strangest times.'

Headlights entering the parking area came through the window.

'Looks like your ride is here,' he said.

'Yes,' I said, 'looks like it.'

I wanted to ask him questions, but was also eager to leave. Seth was on his way to the front door when I came out.

'You all right, Jessica?'

'Yes, I'm fine, Seth. Just fine.'

We got in the car and Seth started to back out onto the old quarry road. As he did, his headlights illuminated the window to Tremaine's office, where I'd just been. Tremaine stood at the window, waving like someone saying good-bye to a departing family member after a pleasant Thanksgiving dinner.

'Suppose you'd like to tell me why you came

out here this evenin', Jessica?' Seth said as we drove toward town.

'Tell you what,' I said. 'I'll trade you a cup of tea for the benefit of your undivided attention.'

Seth turned and raised his bushy eyebrows. 'I take it you have somethin' to run by me.'

'I certainly do,' I said. 'I certainly do.'

## CHAPTER FIFTEEN

I sat with Seth in my kitchen until almost midnight, telling him what had occurred at Lucas Tremaine's séance, and laying out conclusions I'd reached about a number of things, including Matilda Swift's murder. Among many traits I love about Seth Hazlitt is that he's such a patient listener. His only interruption was to help himself to more tea, and to pose insightful questions that helped keep my thinking on track.

'. . . and so there has to be a connection between Matilda Swift's murder and Tony Scott's death a year ago,' I said. 'It happened at the same cottage they'd both lived in for a period of time. It turns out that Jeremy, Tony Scott's son, is Matilda Swift's beneficiary to the tune of a half-million dollars because she's his aunt, Tony's sister.'

'Which would provide the young Mr. Scott

with a motive to see his aunt dead,' Seth said.

'Yes,' I agreed, 'provided he knew she was his aunt and that he was the beneficiary of her life insurance. He's never given any indication to me that he knew who Matilda was.'

'But what about Tony's death, Jessica? It was an accident, wasn't it?'

'That was the official ruling, but my understanding is that the insurance company hasn't paid off because it still considers the fire suspicious. I intend to follow up on that today with Dick Mann.'

Seth grunted and ran his hand over his chin. 'This business about the trademark application on that insulatin' cloth Tony'd been working on when he died. You say a trademark had never been issued because the material was still being tested.'

'According to what Richard printed out from the trademark office's website. I'm more interested in this company that applied for the trademark, Nutmeg Associates.'

'I'd say your fertile mind has been workin' overtime.'

'I suppose it has, Seth, but I can't turn it off. I just know I'm right, although there are a few missing pieces to the puzzle I'd feel better having in place.'

'And you'll keep nosing around until they are, I'm sure,' he said, smiling. 'I'd say you've got yourself a busy day ahead.'

'You're right, which means I'd better get to

bed.'

'A word of advice?'

'Does that surprise me?' I asked, laughing.

'Shouldn't. Jessica, there's been a brutal murder in Cabot Cove, and the perpetrator of that murder hasn't been apprehended. Which means, of course, that if that individual knows you're getting close to identifying him, or her, he or she is likely to become a little upset with you.'

'I've thought of that.'

'My advice is to make sure Mort Metzger is involved every step of the way. You may write best-selling murder mysteries, and you may have found yourself solving real murders over the years—too many for my comfort, I might add—but you aren't prepared, or equipped, to protect yourself from a real murderer.'

'Good suggestion, Seth,' I said, 'I'll catch up with Mort in the morning—it's already morning, isn't it?—and tell him what I've told you, fill him in on my plans.'

'That's what I wanted to hear, Jessica. Think I'll take myself home now.'

*    *    *

Sleep was out of the question, and I didn't try to force it. I dressed for bed, but instead of heading for the bedroom, I settled in the library, where I seem to do my best thinking. I'd turned the heat down when I left the house, and now it was cold, so I built a fire in the fireplace; the heat it generated, coupled with the warm orange glow of the flames, dissipated the room's chill.

Now comfortable, I concentrated on what had been going through my mind all day and into the evening.

The puzzle I'd mentioned to Seth took visual shape on my desktop, as though an actual jigsaw puzzle were there. Each piece represented something I'd learned since the murder of Matilda Swift on Halloween night at Paul Marshall's estate. Most of the puzzle was starting to fit together—Erica, Paul, Jeremy, Tremaine, Robert Wandowski—but there were two pieces missing. My visualization wrote names on those two pieces—Artie Sack, the gardener, and Warren Wilson, Marshall-Scott Clothing's vice president.

I leaned back in my chair and stared at the fire. It had a soothing effect. When it had burned down to glowing embers, I padded down the hall to my bedroom and knew I'd finally be able to sleep. But what I wanted more, as I slipped out of my robe and slippers and climbed beneath the covers, was for the rest of the night to go quickly.

*       *       *

'Joe? It's Jessica Fletcher.'

'Good morning, Jessica,' attorney Joe Turco

said. 'What's this I hear about you becoming one of my client's clients?'

'Pardon?'

He chuckled. 'Lucas Tremaine. He tells me you joined the séance last night.'

'That isn't exactly accurate. I was there as an observer but—'

'No need to explain, Jessica. If you're uncomfortable about it, I promise my lips arc sealed.'

'I'm not uncomfortable, Joe. I—it doesn't matter. You said you'd check on a corporation I'm interested in buying stock in, Nutmeg Associates.'

'Right. I did check it. It's incorporated in Vermont, a privately held corporation so no details are available. Is it going to be a hot stock? Should I buy some when it goes public?'

'Ah, I really don't know. You don't know who's behind the company?

'Sorry, no names.'

'Well, thanks, Joe. I appreciate the effort.'

'Any time. Say, tell me, what's one of his séances like? I figure I should know, being his lawyer and all.'

I smiled as I said, 'Very impressive. For two hundred dollars you can talk to family members who've died, maybe even a great-great-grandmother.'

'You're kidding.'

'Yes. Thanks again.'

I waited a few minutes before making my

197

second call of the morning. 'Marshall-Scott Clothing,' the operator answered pleasantly.

'I'm calling Warren Wilson.'

'Please hold.'

Another woman came on the line. 'Mr. Wilson's office.'

'This is Jessica Fletcher. Is Mr. Wilson in?'

'I'll see.'

He immediately took the call. 'Jessica, this is a pleasant surprise.'

'I'm not certain if you can help me, Warren, but I thought I'd ask. I'm interested in investing in a company you might know.'

He gave forth that warm, pleasant laugh. 'The only company I know anything about is this one, Jessica, and I'm not so sure about that anymore.'

'I think you're being modest. Warren, is Nutmeg Associates a subsidiary of Marshall-Scott Clothing?'

There was silence.

'Warren?'

'Nutmeg Associates? No, it's not one of our subsidiaries. We have a few divisions, but none called Nutmeg Associates.'

'Well, nothing ventured, nothing gained, as they say.'

'You want to invest in this company?'

'I was considering it.'

'What business is it in?'

'Uh, I'm not sure.'

'Some advice?'

'Sure.'

'Learn all you can about a company before putting any money into it. Too easy to get burned, especially with the smaller start-ups.'

'You're right, I'm sure. I suppose I have some more investigating to do.'

'I wish you well.'

While waiting for the mail to arrive, I called Information in Burlington, Vermont, and received the number for Excel Laboratories. A receptionist put me through to a gentleman who introduced himself as Cameron Douglas, supervisor of the fabric testing division. I asked whether he could update me on the testing of BarrierCloth for the trademark office.

'I'm afraid that's privileged information, Mrs. Fletcher,' Douglas said pleasantly.

'I can understand that,' I said. 'I'm a writer researching my next book and—'

'Oh, I'm aware of who you are, Mrs. Fletcher, and I wish I could help. But my hands are tied.'

'Of course. And I must admit I'm wearing my writer's hat as a bit of a ruse. I have an interest in Nutmeg Associates and was curious whether the patent and trademark would be going through based upon favorable test results. The inventor, Anthony Scott, was a friend of mine.'

'Yes. Well, flammability issues are always problematic when patents are being sought.

Safety is of paramount concern and . . . I, ah, wish I could be more helpful, Mrs. Fletcher.'

'I appreciate being given any time at all,' I said. 'Thank you, and have a good day.'

I couldn't be sure, of course, but his tone said to me that the formula for Tony Scott's BarrierCloth had failed the test, at least the formula submitted to the patent and trademark office by Nutmeg Associates of Vermont, whoever they were.

I skimmed the mail—nothing of particular interest—and headed off on my bicycle for the Marshall estate. Instead of approaching it from the front, I circumvented the sprawling property and entered through a break in a low stone wall, following a narrow path through the cemetery toward Rose Cottage. Rather than go there, however, I veered to my left and went to the barn, where I'd found the shovel and rag containing the blood, which I now knew was the same type as Matilda Swift's. DNA tests would confirm the blood was hers, I was sure, but those results were still weeks away.

I got off my bike at the rear of the barn and put down its kickstand, then came around to the front, hoping to see Artie Sack. My timing was good. He'd just arrived after doing chores up at the main house.

'Good morning, Artie,' I called.

He seemed startled to see me there, avoiding my eyes and mumbling a return greeting.

'Have a minute to talk with me?' I asked.

'No, no, got lots to do here, lots to do.'

'I won't take much time, Artie. We can talk while you work. You know, we've known each other for quite a while now. You always make my small garden look so lovely in spring and summer.'

'Uh-huh,' he said, entering the barn, with me on his heels.

'The sheriff says you were very helpful, Artie. He said he likes you.'

Artie turned and looked at me with sad eyes. I wondered for a moment if he might start to cry, but he didn't, just picked up a rag and started cleaning garden hand tools.

'The sheriff says he understands why you picked up the shovel, cleaned it, and put it away in the barn. You didn't want people to think you'd been careless with a tool. Right?'

'Yes, ma'am. I seen it layin' right on the edge of the cemetery and picked it up real fast. Didn't want nobody to think I'd left it there, careless like.'

'That's one of the things Mr. Marshall appreciates about you, Artie, how careful you are with everything.'

'Try to be, try to be.'

'You didn't know there was blood on that shovel, did you?'

He shook his head energetically. 'No, ma'am, I did not.'

'But you knew Ms. Swift had been killed.'

He said nothing.

'Artie,' I said, coming close to where he stood at a workbench, 'you aren't in any trouble. No one is blaming you for anything. But you can be a big help to me and the sheriff. You'd like that, wouldn't you, to help solve a murder?'

'I would.'

'Ms. Swift didn't deserve to die. She seemed like a nice woman, although a lot of people didn't like her. Did you like her?'

'Uh-huh, I liked her, liked her . . . a lot.'

'I thought so. Did you spend much time with her?'

'Some. We talked sometimes, when I tended to the roses.'

'You do such a beautiful job with the roses, Artie. She must have liked living in the cottage close to them.'

'She liked it, told me she liked it.'

I paused and watched his methodical buffing of the garden tools before continuing. 'She liked to bake cookies, didn't she?'

'Yes, she did, baked cookies.'

'Did you ever have any of the cookies she baked?'

'They were good. Best cookies, best ones.'

'I bet they were.'

I was about to ask my next question when he stopped cleaning the trowel in his hands and started to cry. I put my hand on his shoulder and felt his body quiver beneath his green army surplus jacket.

'Is it that she's dead, Artie?'

He sniffled and said, 'Yes.'

'You liked her a lot, didn't you?'

He blew his nose in the rag he'd been using, then turned it over and resumed his chore.

'Artie,' I said, 'do you know anything that would help me—us—find out who killed Ms. Swift? Wouldn't you like to do that? Wouldn't that make you feel very very good?'

'Ms. Swift liked me,' he said, his voice so muffled I barely understood his words.

'She liked you? Of course she did. Everyone likes you who knows you, Artie.'

'I try to be nice, only people aren't always so nice to me. She was real nice to me.' He turned and looked at me, and a trace of a smile replaced his tears. 'Know what she said to me, Mrs. Fletcher, said to me?'

'No, what, Artie?'

'She said she trusted me, trusted me more than most people.'

'It must have felt good to hear that.'

'Like to be trusted, like it. Made me feel good.'

'Of course it did.' I thought for a moment, then said, 'Did Ms. Swift trust you with secrets, Artie?'

He nodded: 'Uh-huh, uh-huh.'

'A special secret, an important one?'

'Uh-huh.'

'I would never have wanted you to tell anyone about that secret before, Artie, because Ms. Swift trusted you to keep it concealed.'

'Uh-huh.'

'But now that she's dead, I know she'd want you to share that secret with people who can find the bad person who killed such a nice woman.'

His brow creased in thought.

'She'd want that very much,' I said. 'When she shared her secret with you, she had no idea some bad person would kill her.'

'I bet she didn't, no, she didn't.'

'Let's you and I find that bad person, Artie. The sheriff would be so proud of you for helping him.'

Without another word, Artie left the workbench and walked to a far corner of the barn, where he started to move heavy wooden boxes piled on top of one another. When he'd removed the last one, he bent over and came up with what looked to me from where I stood like a piece of plastic the size of a sheet of paper. On closer examination, it was a plastic sleeve containing a typewritten letter addressed to Matilda Swift.

'Did you read this, Artie?' I asked.

He looked sheepishly at the ground and shook his head. 'I don't read so good, Mrs. Fletcher. Get the words all confused, all confused. Ms. Swift said to hide this real good so nobody'd ever see it except . . . except like you said, she died and I guess it's the right thing to give it to somebody like you.'

'Yes, Artie, you did the right thing. Ms. Swift would have been very proud of you, and the sheriff will be, too. Now, I'm going to take this letter home with me. Is that all right with you?'

'It's all right, all right.'

'Good. But I'll be back and let you know how you helped the sheriff and me find the bad person who killed your friend, Ms. Swift.'

'That'll be good.'

He began cleaning tools again, and I left the barn, cycling home as fast as I could to read the letter in my library. I studied it a half dozen times before dropping it on the desk and saying aloud, 'That's it!'


## CHAPTER SIXTEEN

'Peter, it's Jessica Fletcher. Calling too early?'

'For me? You know better.'

Which was true. Peter Eder, conductor of our symphony orchestra, is an inveterate early riser.

'Peter, I need an actress.'

'Don't we all? What do you need an actress for?'

'To play The Legend at a private party I'm

giving tomorrow night.'

'Am I invited?'

'Not to the performance, but you'll certainly be on the guest list for the post-production party.'

'Good. Then I'm happy to help. The Legend? You'll need a tall, willowy type.'

'Preferably, although she won't be close enough to the audience for that to matter.'

'How about Sophia Pavlou?'

'I saw her in last year's *Streetcar Named Desire*. She was wonderful.'

'Sophia will make it big one day. What's the job pay?'

'Pay? I hadn't thought about that.'

'I'm sure she won't charge you too much. You know actors and actresses, always looking for work. I can call her.'

'That would be wonderful. See if she can meet me this afternoon at the theater. I'll have the costume and makeup with me.'

'I'll get back to you.'

He did, ten minutes later. Sophia would be at the Cabot Cove theater at three.

My next call was to the Cabot Cove fire station.

'Is Chief Mann there?' I asked the man who answered.

'Yes, ma'am.' He shouted for Richard Mann, our fire chief, to come to the phone.

'Chief Mann.'

'Dick, it's Jessica Fletcher.'

'Hello, Jessica. Hope you're not calling to have me put out a fire at your house.'

'Oh, no, nothing that dramatic. Dick, I'm doing some research for a new book. The plot involves arson, and I thought you might share a little of your technical expertise with me.' Although Cabot Cove's fire department was small by comparison to those of larger towns and cities, Chief Mann's reputation as an arson investigator was national. He'd been called to many other places as a consultant when arson was suspected, and he seemed to be always attending workshops and seminars to keep up with the latest thinking and technology.

I suppose Cabot Cove is like many smaller towns across America in that we attract top people from every profession and walk of life once they've made their marks, and have decided to seek a slower pace. Dick Mann is a prime example of it, having retired as Boston's fire chief after twenty distinguished years to come to our town and take over our department.

Mann laughed. 'How could I say no, Jessica, once you've accused me of being an expert? What would you like to know?'

'I was thinking about the fire last Halloween at Marshall-Scott Clothing's lab.'

'A hell of a bad fire, Jessica. One of the worst I've ever seen.'

'I hear that the insurance company hasn't

207

paid the key man insurance to Paul Marshall because the fire is still labeled suspicious.'

'That's right. Arson still hasn't been ruled out.'

'By the insurance company.'

'And by me. I've never been able to prove it, Jessica, but all my years of experience and my gut instinct tell me someone deliberately set that fire.'

'To murder Tony Scott?' I asked.

'Probably not,' he said. 'Most deaths in arson cases are caused by some other means prior to a fire. In almost every case, someone is murdered, then the murderer sets the fire in an attempt to cover up the crime.'

'I see,' I said. 'I'm making notes as we speak. It's my understanding that a good pathologist can determine whether someone was alive when the fire broke out. True?'

'In most cases, depending upon how badly the body is consumed. In Tony Scott's case, he was burned as bad as anyone can be, which made the pathologist's job tougher. He didn't find carbon monoxide in the blood, which would be a sign that Scott was alive when the fire overcame him, but he did detect a minute trace of smoke stain in Tony's air passages. That could mean he *was* alive. Always tough when there's conflicting evidence.'

I made another note before asking, 'Dick, if there's this conflicting evidence, why are you still leaning toward arson?'

'I knew you'd ask that. The thing that bothers me about the Marshall-Scott fire has to do with the flash points.'

'Flash points?'

'When a fire originates from a single source—a single flash point—we seldom suspect arson. But when a fire originates in more than a single flash point, the antenna goes up.'

'Was that the case at Tony Scott's lab?'

'Afraid so. There were two distinct flash points, and possibly a third. And there was all that calcium carbide.'

'Meaning?'

'Meaning that from everything I could determine, there was no need for Tony Scott to have had large amounts of calcium carbide in his lab. It fueled that blaze, Jessica, especially when the water hit it. Calcium carbide really goes up when it comes in contact with water.'

'Where does it stand now with the insurance company?'

'They're still balking at paying Paul Marshall the key man insurance. He's been raising hell about it, but insurance companies can be tough about such things. In this case, I'm glad they are, although don't tell Paul Marshall I said so.'

'My lips are sealed. Thanks, Dick. You've been a big help.'

'Sure this is research for a book, Jessica, or

because of the murder at Marshall's place?'

'Oh, maybe a little of both.'

'Coming to our open house next week?'

'Wouldn't miss a chance to ride on that shiny new fire engine of yours. My best to Anne.'

Next on my to-do list was a stop at the sheriff's office, where Mort had just finished a meeting with state police about the Matilda Swift murder.

'Any more leads?' I asked after pouring myself a cup of coffee and settling in across the desk from him.

'Only what we've already discussed, Mrs. F. Hey, what's this I hear about you attending one of his séances last night?'

'What you hear is correct. It was interesting.'

'You didn't try to . . . ?'

'Try to contact Frank?' I said, finishing his question for him. 'No, I didn't, but I was tempted.'

'Good thing you fought the temptation. What's it like, his phony séance?'

'I can tell you later, Mort, but we have more important things to discuss. I think I know how to prove who killed Matilda Swift.'

He'd been leaning back in his swivel chair. Now he sat up straight. 'Say again, Mrs. F.'

'I said, I know how to flush out the murderer, and I thought tomorrow night might be the perfect time to make the

210

announcement.'

His hand went up. 'Whoa,' he said, 'let's slow down here. If you think you know who the murderer is, you'd better fill me in. I am the sheriff.'

'Of course you are, and I'm here to do just that, as well as to ask for your cooperation. I might add we can not only reveal who the murderer is, we can expose Mr. Lucas Tremaine for the fraud he is.'

'Go ahead, Mrs. F. I'm all ears, as the saying goes.'

Twenty minutes later, after I'd laid out for Mort what I intended to do and had enlisted his cooperation, I stood to leave.

'Me and some of my deputies will be there like you want, Mrs. F., but I still say it'd be better to just let me go arrest the murderer.'

'I don't think so, Mort. What we have is mostly circumstantial evidence. Oh, I know, circumstantial evidence is sometimes enough to convict, but wouldn't you be better off having absolute proof, maybe even a confession?'

'Sure. Some slick lawyer won't get anybody off with a signed and sealed confession. Okay, we'll do it your way. Besides, it'll do my heart good to see Tremaine showed up for the phony he is.'

'My thinking exactly,' I said, leaving the office and returning home, where a list of calls to make lay in the middle of my desk.

211

Paul Marshall
Erica Marshall
Jeremy Scott
Lucas Tremaine
Warren Wilson
Artie Sack
Bob and Lauren Wandowski

I first called Paul Marshall.

'Paul,' I said, 'I was wondering if I could borrow your Rose Cottage tomorrow night for a little get-together.'

'What sort of get-together?'

'A party of sorts, I suppose you could call it, but with a more serious purpose. I think it's time we put to rest all this nonsense about the Legend of Cabot Cove, and I think I can do it tomorrow night.'

There was a long pause on his end of the line.

'I might also have some information to share bearing on Matilda Swift's murder,' I added.

'Is that so?'

'Yes. I'm sure you want to see that resolved as much as I do.'

'Of course I do. What time is this little gathering?'

'Ten. There'll be a dozen or so people—Seth Hazlitt, the Mullins from Olde Tyme Floral, the Lerners and others.'

'All right. The cottage is empty, and the police released it as a crime scene.'

'You'll be there, won't you?'

'I, ah . . . all right, I'll stop by.'

'Wonderful. Thanks, Paul. I think you'll find it of great interest. Not so festive as your Halloween party but . . . interesting.'

I reached the others on my list and delivered what was basically the same message, altered somewhat to fit what I considered each individual's needs. Everyone naturally had questions and wanted more information, but I politely declined to offer more than what I'd told Paul Marshall. Erica Marshall was clearly annoyed, but agreed to be there. Lucas Tremaine found it amusing, but said he'd be there, too. I didn't speak directly to Artie Sack, but gave the message to his sister-in-law, who said she would come with Artie. Bob Wandowski was at work, but Lauren said she'd give him the message.

I went to the Cabot Cove theater at three and met with Sophia Pavlou. She was full of questions, too, as she tried on the flowing white floor-length gauzy dress I'd brought with me, and experimented with the greenish white makeup, long gray wig and the strands of green crepe paper to achieve the look of seaweed.

'I don't have any lines?' she asked, disappointed.

'No, you don't have to say a word. Just be

there at the right time, make your entrance and leave—but don't go too far, just out of view of the people with me. Wait until I call for you, appear again, then leave for good. Except do be sure to join us as yourself before you say good night.'

'I still don't understand what this is all about,' she complained.

'Trust me, Sophia. When it's over, you'll know everything. I hope everyone will know everything.'

The phone was ringing when I arrived home. It was Seth Hazlitt.

'Everything set for tomorrow night, Jessica?' he asked.

'Yes. You'll be there?'

'Ayuh. Peter and Beth, too, the Lerners, and I got Doc Treyz and his wife, Tina, to come, too.'

'Wonderful. I don't want to limit it to only suspects.'

'As you said, Jessica, havin' others there will make it less threatenin' to the real culprits.'

'Glad you agree.'

'I have one concern.'

'What's that?'

'What if the murderer doesn't confess?'

'Then it was a wasted evening. But do you know what, Seth?'

'What?'

'I think that when I'm finished presenting the evidence, the person who killed Matilda

Swift won't have much of a choice except to admit to the killing.'

'Let's hope you're right. Sure you don't want me to pick you up and drive you there?'

'Positive. I want you to arrive just like the others. I plan to be there well in advance of everyone else, an hour earlier.'

'As you wish.'

I turned on the TV and checked the weather channel. Perfect. The forecast for the next night was clear and cool, with an almost full moon.

Everything was in place. My guest list was complete, The Legend was scheduled to show up on cue, and I knew exactly how I intended to proceed.

All I had to do now was wait. That was the hardest part.


## CHAPTER SEVENTEEN

Dimitri, owner of our local taxi company, dropped me at the rear of the Marshall estate, next to the break in the stone wall I'd used when visiting Artie Sack at the barn. Going through the old cemetery in daylight is always peaceful and pleasant, and I had enjoyed spending reflective time there over the years. I loved the way many of the centuries-old tombstones had sunk into the ground at odd angles, the sun illuminating their faded inscriptions, the branches of ancient trees dipping low over the graves as though paying homage to those buried beneath the weathered stones. I'd gone there on a few occasions with the Historical Society's classes in gravestone-rubbings; I'd proudly framed and hung one of my efforts in my kitchen.

But it is different at night—it always is. Darkness can turn the most pleasant of places and circumstances into something ominous. Noises during the day go unnoticed; at night, they become louder and threatening. In daylight, wind that causes leaves to flutter on trees is pleasant to watch. Not so once the sun goes down and the moving leaves cast shadows that take different forms. I was glad for the moon, although it came and went as fast-moving black clouds crossed it—darkness one minute, welcome light the next.

I walked through the cemetery quickly and reached the Rose Cottage. I tried the door; it was unlocked, so I stepped inside and reached for light switches I'd seen on my previous visit. One turned on a ceiling fixture in the small anteroom, the other an exterior fixture on the front brick patio.

I went back outside. The exterior light illuminated a portion of the long brick wall on which in springtime prize-winning roses blossomed forth in all their glorious color. Funny, I thought, how such a tranquil, happy

216

place could be transformed so quickly into one of menace. All it took was a brutal murder to forever paint the place a different, darker color than when the red, pink and white roses are in bloom.

I looked at my watch—nine-ten. Fifty minutes until the others were to arrive. I'd wanted to be early, have time to collect my thoughts and go over what I intended to do and say. I went to a green wrought iron loveseat against the brick wall and sat, then opened the large handbag I'd brought with me and pulled out materials bearing upon the occasion. I'd prepared everything the way an attorney might, making notes of what I wanted to say in my opening argument, having the supporting materials arranged in order to accompany each point I wished to make.

Confident that I was ready, I sat back, closed my eyes and drew a deep breath. This moment of quiet reflection was shattered by a yowl from behind me. I leapt from the bench and spun around, dropping the materials I'd been holding and bringing my hands up in anticipation of an attack. I looked up to the top of the brick wall. Peering back at me were two large yellow eyes.

I let out a whoosh of air and smiled nervously. It was the big black cat that belonged to Matilda Swift.

'You scared the devil out of me,' I said, extending a hand to entice the animal to me. It pondered whether to trust me, as cats are wont to do, then decided to, jumping down from the wall and rubbing against my leg. I reached down and stroked its smooth furred head. It followed as I picked up what I'd dropped and returned to the bench, then hopped up beside me.

'You're a big, mean-looking fellow,' I said, 'but you're just a softie, aren't you.' A loud purr was the answer.

I remembered the day this cat had jumped onto Artie Sack's shoulder, and how I'd winced at the thought of its claws digging into him. As it climbed on my lap, I caressed the smooth pad of its front paw in my hand.

As quickly as it had befriended me, the cat suddenly jumped off my lap and disappeared into the shadows.

I checked my watch again—nine-twenty. Time was dragging. I decided to go into the Rose Cottage again and turn on additional lights in the event we ended up inside. Beyond the foyer, it was pitch-black. I remembered there were two floor lamps in the living room, and felt my way into the room to a corner where one had been positioned next to a recliner. The chair was silhouetted against moonlight through a window. I touched the chair and was about to reach for the lamp when it came on, causing me to jump back.

'Good evening, Mrs. Fletcher,' Lucas Tremaine said from the chair.

218

'Good Lord, you frightened me to death!' I said.

'I hope that won't be the case tonight.'

'What are you doing here?'

'Resting, contemplating this evening you've prepared for us.'

'You weren't supposed to be here until ten.'

'I'm habitually early, Mrs. Fletcher, catching the worm and all that. I see you are, too.'

He got up and went to a window that overlooked the rear of the cottage. 'Perfect night for The Legend to pay a visit,' he said, his back to me.

'I suppose it is,' I said, not meaning it, but also not interested in debating it with him.

He turned. His crooked smile was unnerving. 'I understand you've taken it upon yourself, Mrs. Fletcher, to dig into Matilda Swift's death.'

'Yes, I'm interested,' I said.

'What have you come up with?'

'I'll get to that when the others arrive.'

'Ah, I like your style, Mrs. Fletcher. Build up the suspense the way you do in your books.'

'But in this case we're talking about real murder, aren't we, Mr. Tremaine?'

'Oh, yes, we certainly are. Much more intriguing than murder created in the mind of a novelist. Ever have one of your fictitious victims be someone like Matilda Swift?'

'A female murder victim? Of course.'

'Matilda wasn't just a "female murder

219

victim," Mrs. Fletcher. She was of another dimension.'

I couldn't help but laugh. 'Really, Mr. Tremaine,' I said, 'you can spare me your claim that she was some sort of spirit, less than human.' As I said it, I thought of the photos of Matilda that Richard Koser had shown me in which Matilda was out of focus while everything around her was razor sharp.

Tremaine returned to where I stood next to the chair. 'Do you feel her?' he asked.

'Feel whom?'

'Matilda. She's here. You can physically take the life of someone like her, but her spirit can never be extinguished. That's what makes her, and others like her, so different. Like your famous Legend of Cabot Cove. I'm looking forward to seeing her tonight.'

'So am I,' I said, thinking of the actress Sophia Pavlou, and wondering what Tremaine's reaction would be to seeing her emerge from the cemetery. Interesting, I thought, that he obviously believed The Legend would make an appearance. Had *he* hired an actress to play The Legend? That was the only way The Legend would join us, and I felt smug at being the one who knew it.

We both looked toward the front door at the sound of voices from outside.

'Ah, the rest of the guests arrive,' Tremaine said, arching his back against an unseen pain and stretching his arms in front of him. 'It's show time!'

'Anybody home?' Doug Treyz asked through the open front door.

'Doug, Tina,' I said, joining them on the patio. 'You're the first to—well, you're among the first to arrive.'

Tremaine came up behind me.

'Do you know Lucas Tremaine?' I asked my dentist and his wife.

'No,' Tina said, 'but we've certainly heard a lot about you, Mr. Tremaine.'

'All highly favorable, I assume,' said Tremaine. The Treyzs didn't respond.

Seth Hazlitt and Ed and Joan Lerner appeared. Right behind them were Paul and Erica Marshall, Warren Wilson and Jeremy Scott, who'd come down the road from the main house.

I mentally ran over the guest list.

All accounted for with the exception of Artie Sack and Bob Wandowski. That was partially rectified when Artie and his sister-in-law approached from the direction of the barn, Artie following her like a child seeking protection behind a mother.

Also missing were Beth and Peter Mullin, but I wasn't worried about them. Their presence would be welcome, but wasn't necessary. I glanced in the direction of the cemetery and wondered whether Sophia Pavlou had arrived yet, dressed and made up like the Legend of Cabot Cove. She was a pro;

I didn't doubt she'd be there at the appointed time.

'Is this a second Halloween party?' Joan Lerner asked. 'If I'd known you usually have two, I would have been happy to host the second.'

'We don't usually, Joan,' I said, 'but this is a special occasion.'

'And I'd like to know just what the special occasion is,' Paul Marshall said. He wore a houndstooth sports jacket with patches at the elbows, shirt, tie and highly polished ankle-height boots. He glared at Lucas Tremaine, who stood with his arms folded, a satisfied grin on his face. 'And what is this nut doing here?'

'The founder of S.P.I.,' I explained, 'has predicted that the Legend of Cabot Cove will make an appearance tonight.' I turned to Tremaine. 'Isn't that right, Doctor?'

'Aha,' he said, 'you've decided to afford me my proper credential, *Doctor* Tremaine. Thank you.'

'The Legend of Cabot Cove is bunk,' Jeremy Scott said, guffawing. 'What kind of party is this?'

'It's a solve-the-murder-mystery party,' I replied.

Jeremy's smile faded. 'If you know something about who the murderer is, Mrs. Fletcher, please lay it out for us.'

'I intend to,' I said, 'but we're missing someone.'

'Who?' Paul Marshall asked.

'Robert Wandowski.'

'Is he the murderer?' Warren Wilson asked.

'I'd prefer to wait until—' I saw Wandowski and his wife approaching from the direction of their cottage. 'Here he is now,' I said.

'What's this all about?' Wandowski asked gruffly.

As the Wandowskis joined the crowd, Beth and Peter Mullin also arrived; Beth carried a large basket of fall flowers. 'Sorry we're late,' said Peter, 'but we had a last-minute order to fill.'

Beth handed me the basket.

'What's this for?' I asked.

'The party. I thought they'd make a nice table decoration.'

'That's sweet,' I said. 'Thanks, but we won't be having a table, I'm afraid.' I took the basket to the brick wall and placed it on the ground, then returned to where everyone was gathered in a semicircle on the front brick patio.

'I'm sorry to say that many of you have been lying,' I said.

'Lying?' Paul Marshall demanded. 'Are you accusing *me* of being a liar?'

'Let me finish, please, Paul. When I said many of you have been lying, I mean about Matilda Swift. And one of the liars here is the murderer.'

There was absolute silence as my 'guests' looked around at one another and then back at me. There was a subtle shifting of bodies; each was wondering if he or she was standing next to a killer.

Wandowski spoke up. 'Well, I'm not a liar.'

'Ah, Mr. Wandowski.' I turned to the big man standing next to his wife. 'You had motive and opportunity.'

'How do you figure that?'

'You told me and the sheriff that you'd come to the party alone, and that your wife had to stay in your cottage for the entire evening to care for Julie.'

'Well . . . I wasn't anywhere near . . . I mean . . .' Wandowski trailed off.

I took the photograph of Lauren Wandowski that Richard Koser had taken and held it up, like a lawyer presenting a piece of evidence to a jury. 'That's you, Lauren, in a moose costume. Pictures don't lie, unless they've been doctored, and I assure you this one hasn't been.'

'I told you when you brought that to our cottage that I was only there for an hour,' Lauren said, her voice breaking. 'I just wanted to get out of the cottage and have some fun for a few minutes.'

'When did she come to the cottage?' Bob demanded.

'You said you'd have your husband tell the sheriff about having left the party,' I said.

'I—'

'Shut up,' her husband said.

224

She ignored him. 'It wasn't fair, his getting to go and not me,' she continued, 'so I made him come home, and I got into his moose costume. It was too big, but I didn't care.'

'I'm not being critical of you for coming to the party, Lauren,' I said. 'But it does mean your husband was away from the party during the time Matilda Swift was murdered—and we know he was extremely angry at her, not only because your daughter visited her that day without telling you, but because Matilda was a stranger here, like Dr. Tremaine. She was someone others gossiped about.'

Joan Lerner pointed at Wandowski. 'I saw you downtown the other day bragging you were going to run Tremaine out of town.'

Erica Marshall added, 'And you've been walking around saying you hated these newcomers so much you wanted to move from this estate because of them.'

'So what?' Wandowski growled. 'Everybody who's mad at somebody doesn't go around killing them.'

'Not usually,' I said, 'but sometimes they do.'

Before he could respond, I turned to Erica, who stood between Warren Wilson and Jeremy Scott. 'I'm disappointed in you, Erica. You lied, too.'

'No, I didn't.'

'You told me you didn't know Matilda Swift, had nothing to do with her, had never even had a conversation with her.'

'That's right.'

'But you baked cookies with her.'

'I did not!'

'Oh, Erica, I think you did. Little Julie Wandowski recognized you. Why would you lie about something as innocuous as that?'

'Because of . . . him.' She directed her words at her father, Paul. 'You told me to have nothing to do with her, and I didn't want to go against you, but—'

'But what?' I asked.

'But I . . . I just found myself coming here to Rose Cottage. I can't explain it. It was as though there were a magnetic field that pulled me here, a force. I was like a moth, and she was a candle. Oh, God, it sounds so stupid.'

'Not to me,' Tremaine said.

I didn't let him go into one of his explanations about Matilda being some sort of supernatural being. I said to Erica, 'Wasn't it more a matter of not wanting anyone to know you'd struck up a friendship with Matilda, Erica? Because not only were you embarrassed about spending time with this strange woman who'd moved here, you didn't want your father to know that you were looking for evidence concerning Tony Scott's death.'

'Is that true?' Paul asked his daughter.

Her eyes flared with anger, and her voice mirrored it. 'Yes, it's true. Everyone knows the

226

fire that killed Tony wasn't an accident.'

All eyes went to Paul Marshall.

'How dare you?' he said. 'You've been hinting for more than a year that I might have had something to do with Tony's death. The man was like a brother to me, Erica.'

Warren Wilson weighed in. 'Your father is right, Erica. I've heard you question whether he was involved in some way with the fire. He's your own father, for God's sake. How could you?'

Erica turned her ire on Warren. 'It wouldn't matter to you whether my father did kill Tony, would it, Warren? The only thing that's ever mattered to you is my father's money.'

I thought for a moment that Warren might physically attack Erica, and was glad when Jeremy took a few steps in order to position himself between them. Tony Scott's son said, 'Now maybe we're getting someplace.'

'I know you each have your reasons for lying,' I said, 'and even though I'm sure you can justify those lies, I can't help but wonder whether the underlying reason is to distance yourselves from any possibility of guilt in Ms. Swift's murder. If you were innocent, there was no reason to deny knowing her.'

I confronted Jeremy Scott. 'Jeremy,' I said, 'your lies concern me more than Erica's and Bob Wandowski's.'

'What lies?' he said.

'About not knowing Ms. Swift. You were in

227

the Rose Cottage on a number of occasions, including just about the time she was killed. Unless, of course, Ms. Swift smoked cigars. As far as I know, she didn't.'

Jeremy's laugh was nervous. 'What did you do, Mrs. Fletcher, find a cigar in the cottage and automatically assume it was mine? Lots of people smoke cigars.' He looked around at the others. 'What a joke.'

I smiled. 'As a matter of fact, Jeremy, I did find a cigar, and yes, I did assume it was yours, But there's a good deal more than that to indicate that you and Matilda Swift weren't strangers. Blood relatives would be a better description of your relationship.'

The gasp from the group was spontaneous and loud.

'Blood relatives?' Paul Marshall boomed. 'What the hell is she talking about, Jeremy?'

'My question, Jeremy,' I said, 'is when did you learn that Matilda Swift was your father's sister, your aunt? Before or after you returned to Cabot Cove?'

'She . . . this is the first I've heard of it.'

'She was your aunt, Jeremy?' Erica asked, her voice testifying to her disbelief.

When he didn't answer, I did.

'Anthony Scott and Matilda Swift had been out of touch for a long time. They didn't know where each other lived until Matilda read about Tony Scott's efforts to develop BarrierCloth. That's when Tony discovered that his sister lived in Salem, Massachusetts. He got in touch with her not long before he died.'

'Why didn't she just announce who she was when she got here?' Paul Marshall asked.

'Because she didn't come to Cabot Cove to be reunited with her brother's family,' I said. 'She came to Cabot Cove to discover who killed him.

I held up the letter Artie had shared with me, but I didn't pass it to anyone. 'This explains it quite nicely,' I said.

'She rented Rose Cottage under false pretenses,' Paul Marshall said. 'If I'd known—'

'If you'd known who she was, Paul, you might not have spent all that money "renovating" Rose Cottage, would you?'

'What does that mean?' he asked.

'You used the excuse of renovating Rose Cottage to search for the formula for BarrierCloth. Even though you'd been told by Tony—and told by Warren, too—that he'd never developed a working formula, you wanted proof. You never found it, did you?'

'Excuse me,' Warren Wilson said. 'This is all very interesting, but it doesn't have anything to do with me. So that crazy lady was Tony Scott's long-lost sister. So what? I have better things to do than stand around here and—'

'It has everything to do with you, Warren,' I said. 'I suggest you stay a little longer. Mr. Tremaine has promised us a visit from The

229

Legend.'

Wilson shook his head. 'Has everybody gone nuts? The Legend of Cabot Cove? That's just a crazy myth.' He looked at Lucas Tremaine, who now leaned against the brick wall, arms folded in defiance, a smirk on his face. 'Is this one of your con games, Tremaine? You belong in jail.'

'You lied, too, Warren,' I said.

He fixed me in a hard stare. I ignored it and said, 'At the party, you said you'd never been to Rose Cottage since Matilda moved in. Yet you claimed that the scratches on your hand came from Matilda Swift's cat.'

'That's hardly important.'

'But you weren't telling the truth either time. I remembered that cat jumping down on Artie's shoulder and thinking it must hurt to have its claws digging in. But Artie said the cat couldn't hurt anyone. At first I thought he was talking about its disposition. But the fact is, the poor thing has been declawed, so it couldn't have scratched your hand.'

'You're right, Jessica. It wasn't the cat that scratched me. It was . . . I scratched it on a . . . on a wire in my apartment.'

'No, Warren, I think you scratched it right here, at Rose Cottage. As beautiful as roses are, they have very sharp thorns.'

'Why would he be handling the rose bushes?' Paul Marshall asked. 'He's no gardener.'

'He was looking for something,' I said.

'Looking for what?' Marshall asked.

'He was hoping to find this,' I said, again holding up the letter Artie Sack had recovered for me from the barn. 'Maybe if I read it, things will become clear.'

'Go ahead, Jessica,' Seth said.

I adjusted my half-glasses on my nose, cleared my throat and began reading:

Dear Matilda:

It's unfortunate that we have found each other so late in our lives. I would have enjoyed knowing my sister years ago, when things in my life were happy and relatively carefree. But that is no longer the case, and I'm compelled to write to you in the hope that you will do the right thing by my son, Jeremy, should anything happen to me.

I don't say this as a doomsayer. But certain events have recently taken place that cause me to question whether my life might be in danger.

Paul Marshall interrupted by laughing. 'Poor, paranoid Tony,' he said, shaking his head. 'He was accident-prone, as anyone who knew him can testify to. The last six months of his life, he really started going off the deep end, imagining someone was out to get him, run him over, drop something on his head.'

'You know what they say,' Seth said in response. 'Just because you're paranoid doesn't mean they aren't following you.' To me he said, 'Go on, Jessica. Continue reading.'

As I've told you, I've been working for more than a year on a formula for a new lining for our outerwear that is warmer and lighter than our competitors'. I thought I'd been successful, but there was the problem of it not meeting federal flammability standards. I've been working day and night to solve this problem, and only last night came up with the answer. That should be considered good news.

Ordinarily, I would have immediately shared this news with my partner, Paul Marshall, but I've grown not to trust him.

I glanced at Marshall, whose expression said he'd heard quite enough and was about to leave. 'Please stay, Paul,' I said. Confident he would, I continued.

Paul has brought in a new VP named Warren Wilson. Warren and I have become friends, and from what he's told me, my distrust of Paul is certainly justified, particularly where the formula for BarrierCloth is concerned. I decided that I needed some way of protecting myself and the formula, and have turned to Warren in this regard.

'What the hell is he talking about?' Paul growled at Warren, who averted his boss's eyes.

'I think it will be explained shortly,' I said, picking up in the letter where I'd left off.

Warren and I have entered into a business partnership. In return for one half ownership in my formula for BarrierCloth, he has given me $300,000, and has arranged to seek a patent and trademark through a venture capital company of his own in Vermont, Nutmeg Associates.

Paul interrupted my reading again by shouting at Warren and shaking a finger for emphasis. 'I'll have you arrested, Wilson, for fraud and theft of company secrets.'

Wilson, to my surprise, took steps toward Paul, rather than backing away under his verbal attack. 'Tony was right,' Warren said, thrusting his chin at Paul. 'You would have stolen the formula and cut him out. I was protecting Tony. I only wish I could have protected him from murder—*his* murder in that fire.'

Jeremy sarcastically applauded Warren's speech, causing the beefier Wilson to make a fist and shake it at Tony Scott's son.

'No sense becoming upset, Warren,' I said. 'But I must admit I'm having trouble understanding your allegiance to Tony Scott.'

'What do you mean by that?' he asked.

'It seems from Tony's letter to his sister that he threw you, his new partner, a nasty curve,' I said. I didn't give him a chance to reply and started reading again.

I suffered quite a bit of guilt, Matilda, selling the formula to someone other than my partner of many years. I sometimes wonder whether I'm too suspicious of those around me, too quick to question their motives. But I know I'm right in this case if I'm to benefit myself from my work, and see to it that those I love reap the rewards after I'm gone. That's why I did what I had to do with Warren Wilson after taking the money from him.

'What did he do to you, Warren?' Erica asked.

'Nothing. He was obviously going mad. You can tell from this stupid letter that he was nuts.'

'Paranoid perhaps,' I said, 'but maybe he had cause to be. Let me finish the letter.'

Because Warren was willing to sell out Paul Marshall, I became convinced he'd do the same to me. So, I provided Warren

234

with a fake version of the formula, one I knew wouldn't pass muster in any lab. Warren has submitted the unworkable formula to the patent and trademark office, which, as a huge bureaucratic agency, will probably take years to come to a decision.

In the meantime, I intend to hide the working formula I perfected last night until I've had a chance to decide how best to protect it so that Jeremy will benefit one day. The cottage I live in on Paul's estate is called Rose Cottage. It has a long brick wall covered with prize-winning roses. I love it here. It's peaceful and quiet, things I treasure in life. If I should die, you'll be able to find the new formula, the one that works, in that wall, behind the bricks. Artie the gardener will show you where. I trust him implicitly. Should anything happen to me, I beg you to come here, retrieve the true formula, and take all necessary steps to secure the proper trademark for it and arrange for Jeremy to reap whatever rewards there might be.

But I ask one thing of you, Matilda. Do not let Jeremy know that you are his aunt, or that he stands to benefit from the formula, until the truth has come out.

Thank you, Matilda. It gives me considerable comfort that I can ask this of someone whose blood I share, rather than entrusting it to strangers who can never be trusted.

Your loving brother, Tony

When I finished reading, I slowly lowered the letter and took in everyone's faces. To say shock was written on most of them would be an understatement.

'The formula for BarrierCloth,' I said. 'The *true* formula. Must have been upsetting, Warren, when you found out you paid a lot of money for the wrong formula.'

Paul Marshall grabbed Warren's arm. 'You told me Tony said he'd never perfected the formula.'

I continued, still looking at Warren. 'The formula you'd registered for trademark protection under Nutmeg Associates, your Vermont corporation, instead of Marshall-Scott, didn't work, did it, Warren?'

Paul roared. 'Nutmeg Associates?'

Warren turned to Paul. 'Don't listen to her, Paul. She's as crazy as the Swift woman was. I was protecting you. Tony Scott was a bad guy. He sold out everybody.'

'Hey, that's my father you're trashing,' Jeremy shouted.

Marshall glared at his vice president. 'Protecting me? By registering the formula in another corporation's name?' He looked at me. 'Go on, Jessica, I've suddenly developed a keen interest in what you're saying.'

But Warren spoke first. 'I see what you're getting at, Jessica. Of course. Paul here found out that his partner had sold him down the river. So he killed him and set that fire to cover it up.'

'I knew it,' Erica said, beginning to cry.

'I don't think so,' I said. 'No, Warren, I think it was you who killed Tony Scott in anger over having given him all that money for a worthless formula. You figured you had the true formula, and told Paul that Tony hadn't been able to perfect it. But then you discovered through the lab in Vermont—Excel Laboratories—that it would never pass a government flammability test. What happened then, Warren? Did you demand the money back from Tony? Did he balk? He certainly was more cunning than his reputation as a mild-mannered, accident-prone inventor would suggest. I wouldn't blame you for being angry at him but—'

'I didn't kill anybody,' Warren said.

'What about Ms. Swift?' Seth asked.

'Yes, what about her?' Warren said, turning and pointing to Jeremy. 'He's the one who benefits from her death.'

'Jeremy didn't know Matilda was his aunt,' I said. 'He had no idea that his father had written the letter to Matilda, or that Matilda, his aunt, had taken out a half-million-dollar life insurance policy before coming here, with

Jeremy as the beneficiary.'

'A half million?' Jeremy said, incredulous.

'No,' I said, 'Jeremy didn't have a motive to kill Matilda because he wasn't aware of his relationship to her.' I fixed my eyes on Warren. 'You searched Rose Cottage on Halloween night, looking for the real formula, Warren. Matilda Swift caught you, and when she ran for help, you followed her outside, grabbed the shovel and killed her.'

'You're crazy. You can't prove a thing.'

'I disagree, Warren,' I said. 'Everyone, it seems, has been operating out of greed and paranoia. This distinguished family and its business perhaps isn't as distinguished as it appears on the surface. But greed and paranoia aren't crimes. Murder is. You're the only one, Warren, who truly had reason to kill Tony Scott and then Matilda Swift. And now that your business relationship with Tony Scott has been revealed, and your lies about never having had any contact with Matilda are factored in, I think Sheriff Metzger and his law enforcement colleagues won't have much of a problem convincing a jury of your guilt.'

Warren's expression turned from defiance to panic, and he looked as though he might bolt. I peered into the darkness toward the rear of the cottage. 'Sheriff,' I shouted, 'I think it's time for you and your deputies to join the party.'

Mort, followed by Wendell and Harold,

emerged from the shadows.

'Got anything to say, Mr. Wilson?' Mort asked Warren.

'Go to hell,' he said.

'How could you?' Erica said. 'You kept telling me you knew my father had arranged for Tony to be killed in the fire. And I believed you.' She turned to her father. 'I'm so sorry,' she said.

Mort's deputies moved to either side of Warren. 'You're under arrest,' Mort said as Harold and Wendell each took one of Warren's arms.

Then Mort looked at me. 'Wait a minute,' he said. 'Where's the real formula you've been talking about?'

I looked to where Artie Sack had stood silently at his sister-in-law's side. 'Artie,' I said, 'it's time for you to uncover the formula.'

The small crowd was silent.

Artie stepped forward. He walked to the wall and reached behind one of his cherished rose bushes, wresting several bricks from their places. He returned to us, carrying a narrow plastic tube. Inside, I knew, was the formula Anthony Scott had developed for BarrierCloth.

'Thank you, Artie,' I said, taking it from him and handing it to Jeremy Scott. 'This is yours, Jeremy. It's what your father wanted.'

'Hold on a second,' said Paul Marshall, stepping forward and grabbing the formula from Jeremy. 'Tony and I were partners. This formula belongs to the company.'

Warren suddenly broke free of Wendell and Harold's grip, yanked the formula from Paul and ran in the direction of the cemetery. Pandemonium broke out, everyone shouting to the deputies to catch the killer, some running to help.

But as Warren reached the first gravestone, The Legend rose before him. Her face was greenish gray in the pale moonlight, her white dress billowing in the breeze. She raised her white arms as Warren neared. He screamed and froze. The deputies were upon him seconds later and marched him to a patrol car. Mort retrieved the formula and handed it to Jeremy.

With a collective sigh, the crowd turned back to me.

'Was that The Legend?' Joan Lerner whispered. 'Not that I believe in such things but—'

'I was told by Dr. Tremaine that she would, indeed, join us tonight, at this spot.' I turned to Tremaine. 'Isn't that right, Dr. Tremaine?'

'True,' he said, stepping forward. 'I had a vision, and I trust my visions.'

'Poppycock,' Mort Metzger said.

'A vision, my foot,' Ed Lerner said.

'I predicted terrible plagues would descend on Cabot Cove, and look what's happened.' Tremaine was smug.

'Oh, those plagues, Doctor,' I said, 'you mean like all the dogs howling in Cabot Cove?'

'Exactly.'

I held up a whistle, the kind with a high-frequency sound that only canine ears can detect. 'I found this dog whistle on your desk the night of the séance. Using this and the enormous public address system you have installed at your headquarters, you must have reached every dog for miles around.'

'Well, I predicted The Legend's appearance, didn't I?'

I left the group and approached the cemetery.

'Legend of Cabot Cove,' I yelled, 'it's time for you to show yourself to us again.'

Silence fell as everyone waited for what would happen next. There was nothing. I called again for Sophia Pavlou to make her appearance. I couldn't believe it. Where was she? How could she let me down this way? I turned in disappointment and was returning to the group when Deputy Wendell Watson said, 'There she is!'

'That's right,' Peter Mullin said. 'Look!'

'I see her!' Beth Mullin said.

I turned. Standing there in the cemetery—almost floating was more like it—was Hepzibah Cabot, the Legend of Cabot Cove, only I knew it was the actress, Sophia Pavlou. I smiled to myself. 'Good job, Sophia,' I muttered under my breath. 'Go on now, walk away, disappear, the way I instructed you.'

She was gone.

'I told you,' Tremaine said, triumph in his voice. 'Maybe now people will believe me in this town.'

'Oh, Dr. Tremaine,' I said, 'I wouldn't be too quick to claim credit for anything.'

I faced the cemetery. 'Legend, come join us.'

'What are you saying?' Tina Treyz said to me. 'You're asking the Legend of Cabot Cove to join us? I saw her.' She turned to her husband, Doug. 'I saw her,' she repeated.

'So did I,' he said.

I called again. And again. But Sophia didn't appear. She must have forgotten she was to remain for a curtain call—to show up Lucas Tremaine for the fraud that he was.

'Well,' I said, 'it doesn't matter. I can explain. What you saw wasn't The Legend. It was an actress I hired to play the part of The Legend. In fact, some of you know her, Sophia Pavlou. I asked her to dress up like The Legend. Her timing was really wonderful, wasn't it.'

'Well, now, that certainly explains it,' Seth Hazlitt said. 'Should put to rest all the silly talk about there even bein' a legend.' He looked Tremaine's way. 'Should convince folks to stop givin' you money, sir, for bein' conned by you. Might be time for you to pack up your things out on the quarry road and find another place to hang out your bogus shingle.'

242

# CHAPTER EIGHTEEN

Seth drove me home from the Marshall estate. I'd been filled with adrenaline at Rose Cottage, but now I felt as though a plug in my body had been pulled and every ounce of energy had drained from it.

'You've got messages,' Seth said, noticing the flashing light on my answering machine.

'I don't want to talk to anyone, Seth. I was going to make a cup of tea, but I think some brandy is what I really want.'

I poured a snifter for both of us, and we settled in my library.

'You sure put Tremaine in his place,' Seth said, lifting his glass in a toast, which I returned. 'To say nothing of putting Mr. Warren Wilson in his place, too—prison.'

'I feel pretty good about it all,' I said. 'I'm glad Paul Marshall wasn't behind Tony Scott's death, or Matilda Swift's, although he wanted that formula for himself. I think that's pretty obvious. Warren Wilson knew that, went after it, but got greedy. Maybe he planned to sell the trademark back to Paul for a hefty price.'

'Wilson thought he'd get Erica in the bargain,' Seth said, chuckling.

'Not a match made in heaven, Seth. But Jeremy might make things turn out all right if he and Paul can come to an agreement. After

243

all, Jeremy has a stake in the company, and I think he might want to take on Paul's daughter, too.'

I sighed. 'This whole episode revealed a less than flattering side to the Marshall family and its business dealings.'

'Ayuh, that it did. Looks like Tony Scott wasn't such a sterlin' fellow either.'

'Well, he obviously was disturbed. A paranoid genius.'

'Clever devil, that Tremaine, with the dog whistle. Funny how natural things take on a mystical quality when you start believin' claptrap like Tremaine's been handin' out. Know how folks in town started thinkin' that the clothes that have been disappearin' from their clotheslines had something to do with Matilda Swift's arrival here in town?'

'Yes?'

'Seems one o' those runaway kids down at the shelter was helpin' himself to a new wardrobe.'

'That's what happened?'

'Ayuh.'

'But the dog whistle, and clothes disappearing from clotheslines, doesn't explain why the phones became fouled up right after Matilda Swift arrived in town.'

'Had Phil Wick in the other day. Came down with the flu.' Wick is field manager of our phone company's Cabot Cove operations center. 'Said he hadn't seen anything like what happened to the phones in thirty years with the company. Static just started up one day, then stopped as suddenly as it began.'

'Stopped the minute Matilda Swift died.'

'Just a coincidence,' Seth said.

I told him about the photos Richard Koser had taken of Matilda, and how she was an ethereal figure in them while all around her was dear and in focus.

'Just another coincidence,' said Seth. 'Richard must have bought himself a defective roll of film.'

'And Erica saying she was mysteriously drawn to Matilda.'

A grunt this time from Seth, although I judged from his face that he was doing some serious thinking.

I said nothing, and we sat in silence for a minute.

'Well,' I eventually said, 'I might as well see who called.' I got up and pushed PLAY on my answering machine.

The first message was from Joan Lerner, inviting me to another party, a post Halloween, let's-toast-the-solving-of-the-murder celebration. I pushed PAUSE while I jotted down her number, then pressed PLAY again for the second call.

'Mrs. Fletcher, it's Sophia Pavlou. I am so sorry to have let you down, but I couldn't help it. I was getting dressed to go to the cemetery when I tripped and fell. I broke my ankle. I spent the evening in the emergency room having a cast put on. I hope you understand that there was nothing I could do, and that I didn't completely ruin your party.'

She hung up.

Seth and I looked at each other. 'She wasn't there,' I said.

'Appears that way.'

'Which means—'

'Just as soon not think about it, Jessica.'

'I saw The Legend,' I said.

'So did I.'